UNDERCOVER GODDESS

*Book I
of the
No Boundaries Trilogy*

Karen Cavalli

Lavender Press
An imprint of Blue Fortune Enterprises, LLC

UNDERCOVER GODDESS
Copyright © 2020 by Karen Cavalli.

All rights reserved. Printed in the United States of America. No part of this book may be used or reproduced in any manner whatsoever without written permission except in the case of brief quotations embodied in critical articles or reviews.

This book is a work of fiction. Names, characters, businesses, organizations, places, events and incidents either are the product of the author's imagination or are used fictitiously. Any resemblance to actual persons, living or dead, events, or locales is entirely coincidental.

For information contact :
Blue Fortune Enterprises, LLC
Lavender Press
P.O. Box 554
Yorktown, VA 23690
http://blue-fortune.com

Book and Cover design by Wesley Miller,
WAMCreate, wamcreate.co

ISBN: 978-1-948979-40-5
First Edition: September 2020

Dedication

To Lynn Francis Howard,
who introduced me to romance novels

To my husband Tom, who holds on

Other Titles by Karen Cavalli:

Bad Mind

In *Bad Mind*, Karen Cavalli explores the possibility of extraterrestrial beings and what that means for us in this world. As she details examples from her life and others she has encountered, she lays out for the reader what it means to have an encounter with spirit and how it can guide us to a deeper understanding of our reality.

Karen Cavalli writes movingly and well about her life, which has been enriched throughout by otherworldly experiences. She describes her interactions with the people, in the flesh and in the spirit, who have touched her life and who have been touched, in turn, by hers. Some of her experiences are "encounters with aliens." All of her life has been filled with emotionally and spiritually rich events that illuminate the strength and survival of her own spirit as well as the strength of the human spirit.
Don C. Donderi, PhD
Associate Professor (retired)
McGill University, Montreal

Wildly cool. Both academic and curious. This woman knows a lot, and she's good at expressing it in an interesting fashion-she never makes you feel less than, or uninformed. Her work is a discovery that leads you to a milky revelation: there's so much you've missed already. Bad Mind invites you to resee the world you live in. Bravo.
Tom Chiarella

Table of Contents

A half and half's dream 9
Void, too late 17
White giants 29
The clouds escape the sky 37
The ways of the wise reptiles 55
Little pictures on clay chips 63
Sign of the crone, traveler rising 75
Gigante love 85
Bag of ruin 103
Undercover goddess 119
Skeleton shrine 135
Zet rises 145
Eclipse season 153
Beast 173
Epilogue 182

1
A Half-and-Half's Dream

THE ENERGY OF FRUSTRATION PULSED as items in the house shook slightly from the vibrations. "Mave." Her mother's voice rang off the stone walls of their house as she went from room to room calling her name. She would never find her, even though she was close enough to touch. Mave sat in her hiding place, a tiny, secret room behind the library wall known only to her and accessible only by pressing a certain brick in the hearth. That particular brick trembled then stilled.

Through the spaces between the bricks, Mave could observe all that went on in the library where her mother, Audria, spent much of her time. While in there her mother cast astrological charts as part of her job as star counsel to the town's Executrix and sometimes met with representatives of the Ssha, the lizard people. The representative was necessary as the Ssha never left their crystalline caves deep in Ssha Mountain. Instead, they sent a half-and-half, one who was bred between the lizard people and the women of hieros house, human except for their green skin and gills and scales like inlaid opals on either side of their jaws.

"Mave," her mother shouted. She stomped back into the library. She stood still in her trousers and tunic, her hands on her hips, her legs as long and sturdy as a ladder's, her curly black hair tied back. She scanned the room, then her eyes lighted on the mantel. She snatched up the clay chip Mave had given her, on which Mave had painted an astrological wheel in miniature, and closed her eyes.

Her desire to find Mave pierced the air, fanning out in widening circles of searching light. Her mother had never mastered moisovo, the mind-verse through which the Ssha and the half-and-halfs communicated, but the half-and-halfs had taught her how to use desire to find what she wanted. For self-preservation, Mave had learned the antidote early on. She sent her essential self into another mass. This time, she curled into a ball and imagined herself imbedded in the stone beneath her, her consciousness hidden. She felt the warmth of her mother's searching beam shine on her, pause, and then pass on.

Mave relaxed for a moment, letting her self seep out of the stone, but not yet back into her body, which still sat cross-legged. Instead, she dispersed as though she were droplets of mist, floating out of her hiding place and into the library. She dared not tell her mother or Anta, who was her keeper and a member of hieros house, what she was doing. Such a skill was the domain of the Ssha, or the women of hieros house, to whom the Ssha revealed most of their secrets. Even Mave, daughter of star counsel, would not be treated differently for breaking the rules.

Mave floated past her mother, her spirit in the shape of teardrops of mist.

"Mave," her mother said, "I know you're here, somewhere." She inhaled deeply, and the rushing current of air snagged Mave's essence, like a rip tide pulling a swimmer out to sea.

"Where are you, Mave?" her mother bellowed, her exhale sending Mave out on a wave of air before she became sucked entirely into her mother's nose.

Her mother growled in frustration then threw herself into her chair at the table where she plotted astrological charts. Mave flew back to her hiding place and into her body. Her mother's focus shifted from finding Mave to casting her.

Ever since Mave was born seventeen years ago, eighteen in two moons, in the Time of Bounty, her mother had charted her life as it appeared in the stars, noting every planetary transit, retrograde movement, and shift of the moon from house to house. Mave was never exactly clear why her mother was obsessed with her chart. Very little happened in Mave's life. Mave was scared of people, open spaces, and the dark, in that order. She left her home only to ride into the foothills of Ssha Mountain when she ran out of gypsum for drawing on her clay chips. She didn't take part in any of Dia's rituals. She didn't mind the thought of her self dissolving—she was practiced at this now—but recoiled at the thought of the invisible bits of her former self merging with others. Not participating in the rituals kept her intact. She refused to venture out at night and walk the borderlands or engage in other girls' void initiations. Her mother hoped for a change of heart before it was too late to add a second syllable to her name.

As her mother muttered over Mave's chart, Mave sat cross-legged on the blanket on the stone floor and took out a cloth bag that had been tucked inside a crevice. Inside were her clay chips and a small bag of gypsum. She shook some gypsum onto the floor, then spat into the pile to form a white paste. With a small stick, the end of which she'd shaved to a point, she painted the moon in all its phases in honor of the Ssha.

Footsteps sounded in the yard, careful, even, and approaching their door. She rose and peered out of a crack between the stones. It was a man in a purple cloak, an oddly rich color among their usual browns, tans, and beiges. His hair was long, brown, and heavy-looking and bound in back with a string. His skin had a green cast to it, olive almost, and his eyes were dark and warm. His nose reminded Mave of a garden snake's snout, barely rising off his face to make room for his nostrils. He stood at the door, and Mave could see that something was bunched up under his cape, at the small of his back, like a coil of something. He knocked twice, and her mother strode to the door. The door creaked as her mother swung it open, and Mave expected to hear her everyday greeting, but instead her mother gasped and pulled the stranger inside. In a few moments, her mother burst into the library, hurrying the stranger alongside her.

"Be," her mother said. "Be."

Be what? Mave thought.

"Beatt," the man said, as though he had heard Mave's thoughts.

"I know your name," her mother said. "And yes, yes, have a seat."

Mave's mother was flustered, an unusual state for her. "Let me take your cape," she said. "Why in void's name do you have your—"

"I'll keep my cape on," Be said, standing straight. "And please, Audria, no questions."

Mave knew from the squeaks that he had settled himself in a chair near the fireplace.

"What has induced you to come out?" her mother asked. "I haven't seen you in daylight since mother's passing."

Mave paused in her painting. Her mother might mean "mother" as in Goddess, but the Goddess couldn't die; she was

Ssha-created, after all. Her mother might also mean "mother" as in the woman who gave birth to her. If that was the case, was she saying she and this man shared a mother?

"One of our half-and-halfs, Tear, had a significant dream," the man said. "Tear, who's opted to be a she for now, thinks it's a warning and is connected to the influx of the men from the north, the tall ones with their stories of a sun god who lives on a mountain top and casts down lightning bolts. One word echoes in Tear's dream: nephthar."

"Purification?" her mother asked, tilting her head.

"Some sort of flame that purifies, yes, but it's not clear who or what is getting purified. Tear also hears the word 'peat,' but we don't know the word or its origin. Have you heard of it?"

Mave's mother shook her head. "No, never heard of it." Then she smiled. "Perhaps your half-and-half sees atonement in the pale boys' future. The boys will see the error of their sun god's ways and light frankincense to purify themselves of any other bad thoughts. Could that be the meaning of the vision?"

Be shook his head. "Did you know one of these Gigante has joined with Poulx of Apollonoulous' hieros house in some sort of arrangement or union?"

"I heard it was a business arrangement," her mother said.

"More than that," Be said. "Now he helps administer the temple, and what had been the hieros house, the pod, is now just Thras and Poulx' home."

"That is concerning," her mother said as she rose and stretched. "Though it's hard to imagine men being a true threat. Especially these Gigante; I concede, they're tall, but can you imagine the instability of those long spines? They'd break as easily as a reed. What can a bunch of pale boys do against Ssha magic?"

Again, Be shook his head. "They're a part of the change, Audria, but that's all I know right now."

"Hard to believe," Audria said. "Of course you know I'll do whatever's necessary here.," she said with a wave of her hand. "What would you like me to tell my people? We're initiating two young women into the void on the next new moon. I could bring it up then."

"During an initiation?" Be gripped his knees. "Your people take too well to the dark. They leave the world of rational thinking so quickly. Are you sure that's the best time?"

"You worry too much," Audria said. "Have we ever lost a battle to invaders? Remember that tribe of little hairy men from the east?"

Be grinned, then his smile faded as quickly as it had come. "I fear this is much worse." He turned his head to look out the window. "It's always a transition, getting used to the light. How do you spend so many hours of the day in it?"

Audria laughed. "Minimal Ssha blood flowing in these veins."

"Audria, have you talked to your daughter yet?"

Mave stopped her painting mid-stroke and raised her head to stare at her mother through the stone wall, all her attention on Audria's response.

Her mother started to speak, then paused and looked around. "We'll talk another time, my friend. I can't explain it, but I have this feeling that these walls have eyes."

Be stood to leave. His eyes went to the clay chip Mave had given her mother. "What's this?" he asked.

"A gift from Mave," she said, handing it to him.

He examined it as it lay in his palm. "It's very interesting." He raised his head and looked straight at Mave, hidden behind the stone wall. "May I see more?"

"It's all I've got," Audria said. She peered out the window. "The Executrix will be here soon for her daily meeting. You're welcome to stay, but she's a handful. Pushy, bossy, a little thick. Besides, I can't remember the last time Dia's Executrix met someone with Ssha and hieros house blood face to face. Though perhaps you should stay. Give her a little shock."

Be looked startled. "No, I'll go now. Please see if you can find anything in the stars about what's coming. Try looking in places you didn't expect."

"If it's there, I'll find it," Audria said.

2
Void, Too Late

AFTER BE HAD GONE, STRIDING off toward the foothills of Ssha Mountain, that odd bulk around his waist bouncing under his cape with each step, Mave's mother settled back down at her table of charts.

"In the place I don't expect," she murmured, peering at the top sheet of pounded hemp. She laughed to herself. "There's always the sign of the Tromper, but who pays attention to that? Silly old man having a temper tantrum. Oh, for the fun of it then." She turned to the astrolabe at her elbow, studied it for a moment, then looked back at Mave's chart. She calculated its position at Mave's eighteenth birthday, two months away.

She thumped back in her chair. "This can't be; I must have done something wrong," she muttered to herself. "The Tromper never matters in anyone's chart." She pushed the astrolabe aside and stood. "I'll look again later." She stretched, raising her arms to the ceiling. "Mave!" she shouted.

Mave ignored her mother and said to her imaginary giant reptile friends, *Here she goes again*, as she stroked gypsum on the clay chip. *Every week a new catastrophe in my chart.*

Running footsteps approached their door. Mave peered out a crack in the northern wall. Turnip, the Executrix' assistant, come to a lumbering, gasping stop and pound on their door.

"Announcing the Executrix," he called out in his broken voice, as though his throat were a bent trumpet that strangled every note.

"Not now," Audria said, sighing. "I don't know why the Executrix thought putting Turnip to work would be a good idea."

"Void, too late," she said at the sound of crunching.

Mave looked outside. The Executrix thumped up to their door with her walking staff. She wore trousers and a tunic like many in Dia wore, but hers was grayish white, a bloodless color that stuck out among their sands, browns, and greens and hieros house women's red. Her hair was also light, like the color of birch tree skin. Anta liked to joke that if anyone got lost trying to find Dia in the dark, the Executrix could be a beacon.

Turnip opened the door for the Executrix and she marched in. She and Mave's mother pressed their palms against the other's eyes, sealing out the light, signifying darkness as the one true state. Then they sat down near Audria's worktable.

"Lovely night last night, didn't you think?" the Executrix said. "Moon just right, her silvery light keeping everything cool." The Executrix spied the astrological chart. "Any news I should know about?" she asked, reaching out a skinny finger to tap the chart.

"Just a review," Audria said, sweeping Mave's chart aside. "What is it you'd like to discuss today, Executrix?"

"Our next new moon ritual," she said.

"What's to discuss?" Audria drummed her fingers on the table, trying to sneak glances at Mave's chart. "Two young women ready to be introduced to the mysteries of the void and receive the next syllable in their name. Routine. The women of hieros house run the show and you watch at your usual distance, just as a good administrator should."

The Executrix shrugged, her bony shoulders rising and falling beneath her white tunic. "I thought, perhaps, we could make a slight change."

"Oh, really? A change? Such as?"

"Oh," the Executrix said, inclining her head and fixing her face with the look of wide-eyed innocence Mave used with her mother when she was trying to talk her into something, "perhaps conduct it at noonday instead of moonrise."

Audria's eyes narrowed, and she lowered her head like a bull about to charge. "Are you suggesting making a change in Ssha ritual? Remember your assistant, Turnip. He's an example of someone who played with tradition."

Mave turned and looked out at Turnip, who sat against the well, letting the soft rain fall on him. He didn't have enough sense in his big, fuzzy head to tell him to take shelter from the rain.

"Peat, peat," he chirped.

"Hush, Turnip," the Executrix called out.

"You are wasting my time, Executrix," Audria said. She bent her head to the papers in front of her. "Anything else for today?" she asked without raising her head.

With her head bent to her work, Audria did not see the look of pure hatred pass over the Executrix' face, but Mave did.

"Yes," the Executrix said slowly. "Just one question. Has anyone ever seen a member of the Ssha, those who command us to revere the dark of the void?"

Audria slowly raised her head but said nothing.

"Legend has it they once lived among us. I've always wondered why they haven't left behind evidence," the Executrix went on. "A claw. Green scales. A footprint."

"Legend?" Audria said. "That's right, you're new here, aren't you? They lived among us when I was a girl. My word should be proof enough. In fact, one of their members was just here."

The Executrix looked around. "Just as I thought, no evidence."

"They travel in two worlds at once, this world and the other. They don't exist in this dimension as concretely as we do. Executrix, why are you questioning me on such basic details? These are things every child knows."

The Executrix leaned over the desk. "There you are wrong. Just yesterday I overheard two children debating whether the Ssha really exist."

"Careful," Mave's mother said. "An Executrix is no more exempt from the laws of hieros house than Turnip."

The Executrix only smiled, and with a stiff bow, departed star counsel's house, her brittle joints cracking and popping.

Mave watched her mother stand. She was focused on Mave's chart, her face tight with concern. She looked out her window, and, seeing that the Executrix and Turnip were gone, well down the road leading back to the town, Audria rolled up Mave's chart, slung a cape around her shoulders and strode out of the house. She stood in the front yard, shouted, "Red Spirit," and slapped her thigh. In a moment, her chestnut bay galloped around the side of the house from the stable. Audria swung herself on and together they bounded out of the yard and disappeared into the hills leading to Ssha Mountain.

Mave gently pressed the large stone that served as her secret door and slid out into the library. The house was quiet without her mother, though the vibrations she left behind were strong.

Mave took two apples from the kitchen and went to the

stables. Wonder and Oats, two mares who were sisters, whinnied at Mave's approach. Both trotted up to her and nuzzled her, searching for hidden treats. She gave each an apple, then said to Wonder, "Will you take me into the hills of Ssha Mountain?"

Wonder tossed her head in a yes.

"Oats, stay here," Mave said. She curled her fingers into Wonder's mane and swung up on her back.

When they got to the foothills, Mave asked Wonder to wait for her. She crawled into a small cave hidden by a laurel bush growing out over the top of the entrance. It was dark inside, but light shone in at the threshold. Mave was practicing, trying to make herself get used to the dark.

The packed earth was dry, and she crossed her legs beneath her. She took out her clay chips and gypsum and plucked a root from above her to serve as her paintbrush. She mixed the gypsum with her spit and began painting a quarter moon on a clay chip, a gift for the Ssha who were somewhere below her, with their tiara heads and wise ways.

Mave pretended she could speak in moisovo.

Hello, she called in her mind. *I'm here if any of you wise lizards would like to talk. You've been down there a long time. Do you want to know what's been happening?*

A chorus of voices, dry and raspy as a snake's hiss, answered, *Yes.*

The Executrix wants to make changes in a void initiation ritual.

Tell us more, Mave heard in her head, even before she had time to make up the line.

Here's something: the Executrix said she knew of children who don't believe you exist.

A shudder went through Mave, as though it had traveled up from the earth into her. Startled, she sat up quickly and smacked her head on the cave ceiling and the spiny roots that grew there.

She stuffed her chips into the bag, tucked them into a crevice, and crawled out as fast as she could.

Don't go, she heard in her head, not the dry raspy choruses of voices, but a girl's voice.

"Stop it, Mave," she said to herself. Saying her name aloud reminded her she was near the time when a second syllable would be added. And for that to happen, she would have to go into the dark.

Wonder threw her head back and whinnied when Mave came out. Mave rested her head against Wonder's warm neck for a moment, real and solid, no voices coming from it, then climbed on her back and together they galloped down Ssha Mountain and returned home.

After settling Wonder, Mave walked toward the back door of their house, which led into the kitchen. The warm, yeasty aroma of baking bread filled the air. Mave quickened her pace, anticipating the crunch of the crust, and the thick, heavy honey taste. "Anta!" she shouted and ran inside.

Anta stood in a ray of late afternoon sun shining in through the crescent moon window, turning out a loaf of dark bread. She turned her head, smiling. "You should be resting. It'll be dark soon."

Mave shook her head.

Anta knew Mave wouldn't go out once it got dark, but she never quite gave up hope.

It was difficult for Mave to explain, especially to Anta, who had been with Mave for almost all of her life. It was as though the ability to walk from the light into darkness was missing in Mave. It was like someone without legs considering walking—it just wasn't possible.

Anta approached Mave for the greeting. Mave fought the panic as Anta placed her broad palms over Mave's eyes, sealing out the light. Mave tried to focus instead on Anta's sweet smells of baked bread and mint but was almost overwhelmed by a sense of the walls closing in. She pushed Anta's hands away.

Anta's hair was cut short in the style of hieros house women. She wore trousers gathered at the ankle and a jacket with ribbons of fabric sewn onto the flaps so she could tie it shut. She trimmed Mave's trousers and jacket in the same way. Audria's trousers were loose and floppy at the ankle, often dragging on the ground, and she'd had Anta stitch shut her jacket flaps so she could pull the whole affair over her head when she dressed in the morning.

"How's my Mem?" Anta asked, using the nickname she'd given Mave when she first came to her, when Mave was two and her gramia had just died, her mother's mother. Mave had had a helper-father at some point, according to her mother, but Mave had no memory of him before he too died. Unlike most women in their town, Mave's mother had chosen two paths: star counsel and partnership with a mate. At that time, her mother was new to her job as counsel to the Executrix and kept forgetting to feed Mave.

"I'm okay," Mave said.

Anta broke off a piece of bread from the warm loaf and dipped it in honey. She handed it to Mave on a flat metal corver. "How is your mother?"

"The usual ranting and raving."

"Ah," Anta said and opened a cloth bag of field greens and began the slow process of brushing dirt off each leaf. "What was her topic today?"

"Well, first, she talked the Executrix out of changing tomorrow's ritual from night to day."

Anta stopped cleaning the greens and stared at Mave. "What? Changing the time?"

Mave nodded. "The Executrix suggested doing it at noon, when the sun is at its highest point."

Anta sat back in her chair. She frowned at Mave, then after a moment smiled and resumed cleaning the greens. "What else?" she said, as though Mave were telling her a joke.

"The Executrix said she heard two children in the village say the Ssha don't exist."

Anta burst out laughing. "Now I know you're telling me tales."

"I'm not telling tales," Mave said, her feelings hurt. "It's true. I heard it all. My mother even had to warn her."

"Enough, Mave," Anta said.

"You mean you don't believe me?"

"I can't believe the Executrix would do such a thing. And all your mother did was warn her? Why didn't she report her to hieros house?"

"You don't believe me." Tears welled up in Mave's eyes.

"Mem, I'm sorry, but a charge like that is serious. Do you remember what we had to do to the last person not of hieros house who dared to make a change in Ssha ritual?"

Mave nodded. It was a few years back, and the women of hieros house had fixed him so he was little more than a walking turnip. That was how he got his name. Mave never could understand why it was so wrong to question the dark as the only true way, but she didn't dare question it; no one did, or almost no one.

"And besides," Anta continued, "how could you have heard all this?"

It was either give away her secret place or be believed. "I don't want to talk about it anymore," Mave said.

"I understand," Anta said in that voice adults use when they don't. She scooped the cleaned greens into a bowl. "These are ready to steam. Add a bit of water before you put them over the fire. There's also roasted parsnip for you and your mother. The sun's about set, and it's time for me to get back to the house. You're all right?" she asked, putting her hand on Mave's shoulder.

Mave shrugged off Anta's hand. "I'm fine."

Anta swung her cape around her shoulders, sending out a wave of her smells, sweet bergamot, mint, and the warm smell of women. "Til next time," she said, blew Mave a kiss, and was gone.

Mave climbed up on her stool. She could still feel Anta's presence. Mave was mad at her but already missing her.

Oh, Lizard People, Mave called out in her head, as she climbed down and poked the embers of the fire. *I'm up for a chat if you are.*

We're here, she imagined a chorus of voices saying.

Well, Mave began, *you'll never believe what happened*, and let her mind sink into an imaginary conversation with the Ssha as she ate her dinner and the last rays of that day's sun cast the shadow of a waning moon on the wall.

After dining on field greens and parsnip, Mave watched the sun's glow fade from gold to pink, then the violet of dusk. Soon the people in her village would leave their homes and roam the foothills of Ssha Mountain while the veil between worlds thinned. Some would have visions and some would not, but all would experience straddling two worlds, like standing in two rivers at once.

Mave felt safe at the kitchen table, even with the dark closing in on her. The kitchen walls were thick with Anta's spells, keeping Mave and her mother protected. Feeling brave, Mave leaned her head out the window and counted falling stars, numerous this time of year. Then she searched for her constellation, the Crone, a figure in a flowing cape poised between worlds. What it really looked like was a straight line of bright points with a spray of more glittering lights off its back and a bright star at both top and bottom. On the other side of the sky, Mave found the Traveler, her rising sign, a group of stars that seemed to have legs jutting out of it.

Her reverie was interrupted by the brisk sound of hooves clattering into the yard and her mother shouting even before she dismounted.

"Mave! Where are you?"

Too tired to run, Mave rose from the table and struck a piece of flint on the stone floor and lit a candle. She jumped as her mother's boots stomped down the corridor to the kitchen.

"There you are," her mother said, her voice booming off the walls of the kitchen. She strode up to Mave and pressed her palms against her eyes, and Mave's sense of safety dissolved. She fought not to scream.

They parted, and Audria stood with her hands on her hips, her eyes flashing like sparking coals hot enough to melt frankincense resin. Mave tried to think of an escape, but her thoughts fled as her mother's look skewered her to where she stood.

"Draw near, my girl, I have a story to tell. Void, I'm hungry. Any food?"

Mave prepared a corver of cold greens and parsnip and placed it in front of her mother.

"Sit," her mother said.

Mave sat.

"I took a little trip today," Mave's mother said.

"That's nice." Mave looked away.

"Don't you want to know about it? It concerns you," her mother said. "And the Ssha."

"Me and the Ssha?" Mave asked, her voice squeaking out. She sat back in her chair and folded her arms. "Tell me if you want. I don't care."

Audria patted the scrolls on her back. "Have a sniff," she said, cocking her head toward the scrolls. "You can smell the Ssha."

Mave leaned forward, took in a huge breath and fell against her chair back in a coughing fit. "You tricked me," she said, rubbing her nose. "It smells like the latrines."

"Lime," her mother said, and put her nose in the scrolls and took a deep a breath as though they were a bouquet of roses. "Reminds me of when I was a girl, and they lived among us."

"What do the scrolls say?" Mave asked.

Her mother lifted the sling holding the scrolls off her back. "There are prophecies about this time, when the sign of the Tromper with his ax and scale begins to rise in the east, his bright stars blocking out Venus. We've always thought of the Tromper as a kind of joke. A man in charge? No one could take that seriously. But today I saw something in your chart that changed that."

Mave sat silently. They'd been through this before. Audria would discover some awful thing in Mave's chart, go crazy for a while, and then realize she'd made an error in her celestial calculations. She never made mistakes with anyone else's chart, only Mave's.

"Don't you want to know what it is?" her mother asked.

"Whatever." Mave traced a crack in the table with her finger.

Her mother leaned toward Mave and took her hand in hers. Mave pulled her hand away.

"Listen to me," her mother said. "Something is about to happen, and I think you're a part of it."

"Oh, mother, please, not again. Just last month you saw an earthquake coming in my chart, due to hit a week ago, and look, I'm still here. Nothing happened." Mave turned her head to listen to the villagers singing as they left their homes for the hills. "And what about Be's warning that you promised to give the people?"

Audria listened to the singing, looking both dreamy and excited. "I have to go soon. The initiation's about to start." She laid her hand on the smelly scrolls. "We'll talk about these tomorrow. And about Be's warning…" She paused. "How did you know about that?"

The singing grew louder. Something rose up in her mother and, to Mave's eyes, rippled along her skin.

"Stay in tonight," Mave said, pulling on her mother's arm as she rose to leave, the soft singing passing by their house. "Stay with me instead of going into the dark."

Audria looked at Mave as though she didn't know her. "Another time," she said, and blew out the candle. "Tonight is an initiation."

Her mother left then, running out of the door into the night. Mave started out after her, led on by the full moon and its light, but stopped a few yards from the door. Like a dog, her hackles rose. The breath of the spirits whooshed on her neck as she ran back to the house. For a terrifying moment, she could not find the door. She slapped the stucco as though blind and moved from one end of the stone wall to the other, trying to find the door. She fell inside, panting, and crawled into the tiny room where Anta kept clean cloths. There, she curled up into an old cape of Anta's and fell asleep.

3
White Giants

MAVE WOKE THE NEXT MORNING to tendrils of mist snaking into the room. The morning air was cool and moist, but the heat would soon follow. She huddled under Anta's old cape. She would be the only one up for a long time, at least until the sun stood at mid-point, and perhaps not even then. Nightly communing with the other side left people tired, and they commonly slept throughout the morning, but with last night's void initiation they would likely sleep even longer.

Mave tried to imagine herself as someone who found it easy to slide into the dark each night, hear the other world call her name and answer, "Yes." The problem was, she wasn't that sort of person, which made her an outsider in her village and in her home.

Anta would not come today. All the women of hieros house would sleep until moonrise.

The house was quiet without the thrum of active life. She

stood by the library door and peeked in at her mother, sleeping on a pallet near the fire.

"Mother?" Mave said.

Audria didn't move. Mave sat down by the fire, warming herself.

"Mother?" she said again.

Audria was sleeping so heavily she appeared dead. For a moment Mave couldn't tell if she was breathing or not. Mave knelt next to her and took her shoulder. "Mother," she said, louder. The silence grew heavy, weighted as though with bad news. Mave shook her shoulder. "Mother," she shouted.

Audria's eyes flew open, and she stared at Mave, red-eyed, from the world of dreams. "Bear pops and pork pops," she said, then closed her eyes and fell back asleep.

Mave left the house and went to the stable. Only Wonder and Oats stood there, quiet in the chilled morning. They nosed the air, hoping for a treat.

"Later, loves," Mave whispered and patted their necks.

The three of them, horses and girl, looked toward the town. The mist was too thick to distinguish smoke rising from the chimneys. Ssha Mountain rose up in the distance to their left, as silent as Mave and Audria's house. Wonder whinnied, trotted out into the yard, and turned to look at Mave. Oats, behind Mave, nudged her back, and together they walked onto the packed earth in front of the stable. Mave felt as though she were the only human left on their island, as though her town of Dia and nearby Apollonoulous were gone, all humans transported elsewhere. That would be a nightmare for most, but for Mave it would be a dream come true.

Wonder carried Mave on the dirt path into town, and Oats trotted ahead of them. They slowed as they neared the outer ring of buildings. The village was small and compact, three rings of small stone houses and an outer ring of outbuildings where tools and carts were stored, all circling a large grassy knoll. Oats, Wonder, and Mave neared an outbuilding.

Undone by the mysteries of the borderlands, Mave's people slept hard. Most had found their way to their beds, but not all. Three women curled together under a tree, mud drying on their trousers. A man and his dog and his scrying bowl, a black-lined piece of pottery filled with water, were tucked into a doorway. Two women and their brood of six lay strung out like hemp paper dolls at the edge of the knoll. At the top of the mound, a holy place where only women of hieros house could stand, stood Turnip, looking far into the distance, toward the sea and the moon that still hung in the sky.

"You, Turnip man," Mave hissed. "Get down from there."

He jumped, then turned and saw Mave. His jaw went slack, and his shoulders slumped. His fuzzy head bobbed. "Dere," he said, pointing to some far-off point.

"Get down off that knoll," Mave said. Wonder and Oats walked toward him, nosing the air. "If you get down right now, I won't tell."

He dropped to all fours, reared back and neighed, then trotted off the knoll and down the street.

Mave and Wonder left Oats munching grass as they continued to the other side of town. Silence continued to envelope them. Mave squinted as she discerned a figure wavering in the mist. The shape slowly materialized to reveal a person standing between two outbuildings, their back to the broad expanse of land which lay between the town and the sea cliffs. Mave and Wonder neared the figure. The stranger wore a shirt and trousers. Wonder walked through the last curtain of mist and dropped Mave within a few steps of the person whose dark hair was as short as splinters except for the tiara of three points on her head. Her face was green, and gills shadowed her jaw. She was a half-and-half, a him and her. Mave had never actually spoken to one—they were shy and quick as candle-flame on their visits to her mother. Audria sometimes called them in-and-outs.

The half-and-half stood staring at Mave, and she felt a whisper begin at the back of her head.

"This way," Mave both heard and felt as the words slid between her skull bones and into her mind.

Then the half-and-half turned toward the sea, walked into the mist, and disappeared.

Wonder and Mave followed onto the narrow road that led to the fields of wild rye and the bluffs above the sea, where her people rarely went.

Wisps of mist hovered above the ground, and a haze obscured the sun. Squinting, Mave could just make out the back of the half-and-half as she ran ahead.

This way, this way, Mave heard in her head as she and Wonder rode toward the cliffs.

"I'm in trouble, Wonder," Mave said aloud. "I think I'm hearing things."

No, you're not, Mave, voices said, raspy and croaky with cave damp.

Frightened, Mave sent herself into Wonder's mane so no one could find her. Wonder's head jerked back as she sensed the weight of Mave's spirit in her mane. *Harbor me,* Mave sent her thoughts to Wonder.

With a snort, Wonder bobbed her head then continued galloping with Mave's body on her back and Mave's self in her mane. Peering between the coarse hairs, Mave lost sight of the half-and-half. When she no longer felt the presence of raspy voices, she slid out of Wonder's mane and back into her body.

Wonder was running along the edge of the cliffs that

overlooked the sea. Only the women of hieros house were allowed to venture below to the rocks and sand. Anta had once told Mave that even she and the other women of her house in Dia rarely came here. The vastness of the sea bothered them, she said, and they were happier in the enclosing walls of the house and boundaries of their village.

Wonder halted near a bush. While she nibbled, Mave looked out at the sea. She had to resist sliding back into Wonder's mane. The sea spread out wider than anything she'd ever seen. It was unsettling. Who knew what lay beyond it? More sea, perhaps, or more people. None of her people had ever felt a curiosity about what lay beyond it. They could not explore the void here. Too dangerous.

As Mave stared, dreamy now and not so afraid, Wonder lurched to the side. Mave slid to the other side and grabbed her mane to keep from falling off as Wonder bolted away from the cliff and galloped into a thick stand of trees set back from the edge. She came to an abrupt stop and Mave shot over her head, landing on the hard ground.

"For void's sake, Wonder," Mave said, standing and brushing herself off. "You could have hurt me. I'll have bruises for sure."

Wonder shook her head in a weaving way, as though she were tracing the in-and-out path of a bumble bee with her nose. Then she became very still.

"Wonder," Mave whispered, "what is it?"

Mave looked where Wonder's stare was focused. Approaching from the opposite way they had come was a hooded figure, dressed all in white. The Executrix.

Wonder stepped back, deeper into the trees. Mave crouched at her side.

The Executrix stopped at a point directly in their line of vision. She stood with her back to them for a long time, not with the relaxed posture of someone meditating on the sea, but tense and waiting.

Crouched by Wonder's flank, Mave's muscles began to cramp. Just as she was thinking of rising, stretching, perhaps even coaxing Wonder out of the trees, the ground began to shake, as though a hundred horses were barreling toward them. The Executrix turned to face whatever was coming.

Mave crept to the edge of the small stand of trees and peered out. Wonder shrank farther back. Mave could see something huge approaching, rising and falling as it came, like several riders and horses, but twice as high. She thought it must be an illusion. She had once seen Anta create an illusion, an army of women on horseback when the tribe of hairy men had tried to take over their town. Somehow the Executrix must have learned Ssha magic and was about to try her powers here on the cliffs where no one would see her. This was the only possibility Mave could imagine for to explain what she was seeing.

But the Executrix stood still, no chanting, no raising of her arms at the crucial moment when the illusion became real. It was now too real, thundering toward the Executrix.

Mave could not move as the massive, moving body roared to a stop in front of the Executrix. It was as though she had fallen into a dream in the middle of the day. What she saw could not be. They were white giants. Then she realized who they were: Gigante. They who ride. Men from the north.

Two Gigante on their horses, twice as large as those in Dia, towered above the Executrix. A complicated system of leather straps wound around the horses' heads. Large hunks of leather draped over their backs, where the riders perched. A third white giant drove a cart piled with what looked like stacks of dried chunks of grassy earth. The three men had the same wide shoulders and large jaws of the men in Mave's village; but there the resemblance ended—they were twice as big as the Executrix. They were so light skinned it looked as though someone had dusted them in yarrow powder. Two had thick white eyebrows and long manes of pale hair, and one had hair as deep red as a pomegranate seed. All three had skin so fair they reminded Mave of the grub worms that surface in the dirt after a rain, pale and unused to the light.

One Gigante leaped off his horse and stood beside it, his legs planted far apart, as tall as a young fir, talking to the Executrix in a growling voice. Mave could make out only two words in his unfamiliar accent: peat and naphtha.

As he talked, towering over the Executrix, he chopped the air with his big hands, hacking at it, then threw his arms out in sweeping arcs. The Executrix did not seem bothered by his slicing hands. She craned her neck to look up at him as though he were the midday sun. Mave realized that if the Gigante had wanted, he could snap her in two as though she were a stick.

Once the giant finished hacking up the air, the Executrix spoke quietly and in his language. She made no gestures. He nodded, his face serious and scowling.

The hunks of leather on the horses' backs had loops hanging from them, and the white giant stepped into one of these and swung himself onto the horse. With a nod to the Executrix, he and the other man rode away, whipping the animals' flanks. The man driving the cart with the stacks of dried, grassy earth snapped his horse with a whip as well. The horse bolted, wheeling the cart around to gallop after the other two horses. Mave put her face in her hands and dared not look at Wonder. The Executrix turned in the direction of Dia and began walking back, her knees bobbing up like the knobby knees of cranes, then stopped. She stopped, nosed the air. Mave became even more still and for safety shot herself into the sapling next to her.

The Executrix couldn't be using her intuition, Mave reasoned; she wasn't allowed. Anyone not of hieros house could use their intuition at night, when they roamed the borderlands, but not during the day. But then again, the Executrix had trysted with the enemy, which meant she was capable of just about anything.

After a moment, she stopped nosing the air and continued on her way back to the village. Mave watched her bony back slowly disappear.

"Wonder," Mave said, her voice coming out in a croak, "it's safe." Mave turned to see Wonder and for a moment saw only trees. Brown flanks, mane, and peering eyes emerged, and the horse fully materialized. Mave placed her palm on Wonder's neck and with her gentle touch guided Wonder out of the stand of trees. Together they stood at its edge, looking this way and that. Mave's legs felt shaky, and even Wonder had a wary look in her eyes. "I think we're safe," Mave said. She climbed on Wonder's back and whispered in her ear, "Fly, Wonder, the others must know." And together they rode fast and hard back on the familiar road.

4

The Clouds Escape the Sky

IT WAS NEAR MIDDAY. THE sun still simmered behind misty clouds, which seemed to have descended a level, as though they were lowering themselves to the ground, escaping from the sky. Mave imagined a world where everything was turned upside-down, where the clouds would lie on the ground and shoot rain up instead of down. Yes would mean no, and goodbye would mean hello. The sun and moon would continue to rise and set, but the moon would be the sun's weak sister, revered only by wolves and half-humans like Turnip, mumbling into his hands and bobbing his shaggy head.

"Faster, Wonder," Mave whispered, her face close to her warm ear. "Faster."

As soon as they clattered into Mave's front yard, she slid off Wonder and gave her a pat as she trotted into the stable where Oats stood waiting. Mave ran into the house. "Mother," she called. There was no answer. She ran into the library. Audria was still asleep, lying in a tangle of blankets by the fireplace. The scrolls, still bound, lay in a bundle on her table.

"Mother," Mave shouted, stomping her feet. Audria didn't stir. It took a great deal of energy to walk the line between worlds, and sleep was the only cure, giving the spirit time to make the long journey back.

"Mother, please," Mave said, patting her head and squeezing her shoulders, "wake up, please."

She opened her eyes, as she had done earlier, but this time she was staring back at Mave from the other side.

Mave ran back outside and to the stables, where Wonder was rolling in the dirt. Oats was there, along with Red Spirit, watching Wonder. Even Red Spirit seemed worn out, as though he had run, in spirit, with Audria last night.

Mave ran back outside and stood feeling helpless and bewildered in the patch of grass outside the kitchen, watching Oats eating a path toward her through the sweet grass. *What do I do, what do I do...* The litany ran through her head.

Take three deep breaths, came a girl's voice echoing in Mave's mind.

It seemed reasonable enough advice, so Mave took it, letting out huge gusts of air into the hazy midday. Oats and Wonder eyed her.

Don't worry about your mother, the voice continued. *Get to the village. Find Anta and tell her what you've seen.*

Again, a reasonable suggestion, and a good one to follow.

"Oats?" Mave said.

Oats pricked up her ears.

"Let's go," Mave whispered.

They flew down the path to the village, taking a side road that lead to hieros house.

Hieros house was actually a compound of three small, round buildings, one for sleeping, one for cooking and eating, and one for study and ritual. All were stone and built low to the ground. The women of hieros house were small, compact and dense like root vegetables.

Mave slid off Oats and crept around to the front of the smallest round building. There were no windows at hieros house, where darkness was honored at all times. The door was wood and fit snugly in its stone frame. Gently, Mave pushed on the door. It would not budge.

"Anta," she whispered. "Can you hear me? Anta, it's me, your Mem."

No sound from inside. Mave looked around, checking the two other buildings, as quiet as this one, and behind her, down the hill and into the village. The sleepers she'd seen earlier had not moved.

She knocked quietly. "Anta," Mave said. She knocked harder. "Anta," she called, not caring anymore how much trouble this could get her into. She felt beyond that fear, as though seeing the Gigante had cleared it away. "Anta," she screamed, pounding on the door. No one stirred at hieros house.

"Now what, now what," Mave said, clenching and unclenching her fists. "Oats," she called, and Oats left the grass she had been eating and trotted up to Mave. Mave climbed on her back, and they were off again, bounding down the hill into the village.

At the outer ring of buildings, Oats and Mave stopped. Mave's plan had been to scream until someone woke up, but then she remembered the Executrix. She would be awake, but it would not do Mave any good to get her attention. She slid off Oats and crept through the two rings of buildings until she stood in the shadows of a house in the inner ring.

Across the knoll stood the Executrix' house. Mave had no

plan but began to creep toward the house, slipping in and out of houses' shadows. The sun, now past midday, still smoked behind wet, misty clouds.

She crouched below a window of the Executrix' house. To her left lay a woman and a man, their arms and legs stuck out like spokes of a wheel, their chests slowly rising and falling with the deep breaths of those not yet returned from the other side.

"To anyone who will listen," Mave whispered, "help."

Turnip came loping around the side of the house. Just as he spied Mave, the Executrix called out from within the house, "Turnip, it's nearly time."

He froze in place, his back to the Executrix, and looked at Mave not with his usual uncomprehending stare but with eyes shining with intelligence.

"Turnip," the Executrix called again, and stuck her head out of the window above Mave.

Turnip turned away from Mave, reared back, and pawed the air, neighing wildly.

"Not now, Turnip," the Executrix said. "There's not much time. If we wait too much longer, they'll all be returned from their little trips to the other side. We have to catch them just as they make the final step from the other world to this one. And then we'll have the Ssha where we want them, without followers." She laughed to herself. "Then we'll break the back of Ssha magic. Hurry now, Turnip." She ducked back inside and her steps grew fainter as she moved to the back of the house.

Turnip waited a moment then dropped and ran, hunched over, to Mave's side.

"Get away, fast," he whispered, looking this way and that, his fuzzy head moving with a sharpness Mave had never seen.

"Not until you tell me what's going on."

"Turnip," the Executrix shouted from the back.

"Oh, void," he whispered, looking over his shoulder. He swung his head back to look at Mave, imploring. "I'm here to help the Ssha."

"I thought the women of hieros house shut down your mind for breaking the rules," Mave whispered.

"They did, for a time. I knew the rules; I broke them. I knew what was coming. I used word patterning to protect myself. Eventually the words the women of hieros house used were overcome by those I'd set in place earlier."

"I don't want to hear this," Mave said, putting her hands over her ears. "It's blasphemy."

"Maybe you'll want to hear that I acted like I had turnips for brains to protect the women's rights."

"A man protecting a woman's right? That's silly."

"Man, woman—it wouldn't have mattered. I volunteered to serve as an example. That bought us some time and allowed the women of hieros house to continue to think they were keeping the rest of us in the dark. No one, besides a small group of us, had any way of knowing that their spells to mangle thought could be overcome. There are others, you know, out beyond this village and others, who feel as I do, that everyone should be able to use the power of words and of intuition. But we don't want to crush that power, as the Executrix does." He looked nervously around. "There's not much time. The Executrix has made a partnership with the Gigante—"

"The white giants?"

"Yes," he whispered. "We've known about them for some time, and we tried to warn the Ssha, but they aren't open to our kind. We've experimented with moisovo but somehow we couldn't put it into practice. Some of us have tried to get word to the Ssha through the half-and-halfs, who are more open to us. They're having dreams."

Mave remembered her mother's conversation with Be. "But the Ssha do know," she said. "A man close to them, Be, came to our house and tried to warn my mother."

"Thank the void," Turnip said. "There may be hope."

"Turnip," shouted the Executrix, "it must be now."

"I have to go," he said, looking around. "You must get to safety. There's almost no time." He saw something over her shoulder. "She'll help you," he said, nodding at someone behind Mave. "Now go. I'll make enough noise for the both of you to get away safely."

Hunched, Turnip ran alongside the house, then sprang into the back, where the Executrix stood. He began screaming and neighing, and Mave could hear the Executrix trying to calm him.

Mave turned. The half-and-half who had led her to the sea stood there, her hand on Oats' neck. She beckoned to Mave.

Oats let both of them climb on her back, then, to Turnip's whinnying screams, galloped down the street and out of the town, past the people still lying fast asleep.

Her heart beating too hard and fast to think clearly, Mave let Oats take them on the path toward Mave's house. She clung to Oats' mane. Behind her, the half-and-half wrapped her green arms wrapped around Mave's waist and held her tightly against her warm body. Noise crammed into the base of Mave's skull, as though the half-and-half behind her were stuffing her thoughts in. Mave twisted around to look at her. Her eyes were closed, and she looked as though she were meditating as she bounced behind Mave on Oats' back. The half-and-half's face was the color of green mud, and below the gills on her jaw glittered a scale on either side, iridescent like a round, flat pearl. Her nose, like a snake's snout, barely rose off her face, and her mouth was a faint line.

"We'll go to my house," Mave said.

But only briefly, the half-and-half's unspoken words came to Mave.

"Then where?" Mave asked. She twisted around again to face the half-and-half. "Can you talk?"

The half-and-half opened her mouth as though trying to speak, but nothing came out, a fish out of its element. She shook her head. Mave turned back to face the road. Oats was slowing, tiring.

I can't, Mave heard in her head. *But you can, moisovo.*

Mave said nothing. She should have felt fear; she had broken a sacred rule. But for the second time that day, the fear had cleared away.

All that time you thought you were making up conversations in your head. There you were, a human talking to the Ssha in moisovo.

Mave said nothing, tried to think nothing, until her house was in sight.

They crested the hill before Mave's house; to Mave the house looked empty. She leaped off Oats as they clattered into the front yard.

"Mother," Mave shouted.

"Quiet," hissed a voice from the bushes by the door.

"Mother," Mave said, "what are you doing?"

"Waiting for you. Keep your voice down, girl," she said. "Who is that with you?"

The half-and-half and Mave crawled behind the bush and squeezed in with Audria. Her mother's warmth felt good.

"Ah, Tear," Audria said, nodding at the half-and-half.

We got out just in time, came the words in Mave's head, and her mother nodded again. The half-and-half was broadcasting the same thoughts to both of them. *The invaders are in the village*, she went on.

"Not much time, then," Mave's mother said aloud. She turned

to Mave, taking her chin in her hand. "We're in trouble, sweet. The end is near."

Mave burst into tears.

Her mother slung her arm around Mave's shoulders and gave her a brief, hard squeeze. "Don't worry, we've got a plan. You'll go with Tear to Ssha Mountain. You'll be safe there."

"What about you?"

She smiled. "Someone's got to protect the place."

Tear stood. Audria's mother looked at her. "It's time," she said.

Audria called Wonder from the stables, and Tear and Mave climbed on her.

"You'll need Oats too," Audria said. "She's tired but she'll be all right following you."

Audria stood with her fists on her hips. "Your first adventure." She smiled. "Have a good time," she said, as though Mave were going to the fair. "Off you go." With that, she swatted Wonder on the rump. Wonder charged off, Oats just behind her, and it was all Mave could do to stay on Wonder's back as she galloped out of the yard and down the road.

To the caves, Tear said in her head.

Darkness, Mave thought. *Enclosed and sightless like a worm in dirt*. Her stomach lurched and her mind began an uncontrollable whirling as panic set in and normal thought was no longer possible.

Tear placed her palms lightly on Mave's neck. Cool water seemed to flow down Mave's spine, washing away fear and panic. Even as she bounced on Wonder's back, great sighs overtook her and she breathed out big breaths of air, relaxing with each one. She was almost sleepy.

Tear pressed her fingers into Mave's neck, what felt like a laughing touch, withdrawing some of the cool waters. *Don't sleep yet*, Mave heard.

Relaxed and almost happy, Mave nudged Wonder in the direction of Ssha Mountain at the next fork in the road.

They traveled for some time, Mave with her chin nodding to her chest, Tear riding behind her, keeping one hand on Mave's neck and one at her waist. At the foothills of Ssha Mountain, they passed Mave's cave. She patted Wonder to stop.

"I have to get something," Mave said, and slid off Wonder.

Mave bent down and reached into the cave, felt around for her cloth bag, found it, and pulled it out. She sat back on her folded knees and turned to hold up the bag for Tear to see. Tear bobbed her head in a nod then motioned for Mave to join her back on Wonder.

We should go, Tear's voice sounded in Mave's head.

Mave shrugged. She leaned back and stared up at the sky. The sun had finally burned off the hazy clouds and was setting in a blaze, casting the hills in a red and gold glow, appearing as if they were on fire. Her skin recoiled as though flames licked it. A charge of energy shot from the earth into her. She leaped up to standing.

"My mother, Anta," she said. "What's happened to them? To the people in my village?"

We're almost to the first level, Tear's voice echoed in her head, *they'll be waiting for us there. They'll know. Hurry, get on.*

You know what is happening, Mave thought to Tear accusingly and stood her ground.

Tear turned her attention to Wonder, her back to Mave, and Wonder took off in a slow trot.

"Wait," Mave called, panicked at the thought of being out here alone. She ran after them, and Wonder slowed enough for Mave to jump on.

They went deeper into the foothills than she'd ever ventured. Even though Mave had her cave, she always kept her home in sight on her rare ventures.

Bathed in the indigo light of dusk, they made their way to the foothills where evening star bugs glittered among the olive trees. Once they reached the foothills, Wonder carried them up to the lowest ridge.

At first Mave didn't see the caves. All she saw were a line of trees against the black rock of the foothills. As they got closer, Tear reached over her shoulder and pointed. Following her finger, Mave could just make out darker slits between the trees, narrow ovals about her height.

Mave and Tear slid off Wonder. "Wait for us, Oats, Wonder," Mave said, patting their necks. Oats rolled her eyes nervously in the direction of the village and tossed her head. "I know," Mave whispered. "There's nothing we can do."

Mave followed Tear to a cave entrance on the end. Grass and weeds grew at the mouth of the cave, covering it like a beard. Mave touched the plants as they stepped in. They were cool and crunchy. Mave entwined her fingers in the growth and stood there while Tear brushed past her and stepped through the slender entrance. Swallowed by the dark, Tear disappeared. A moment later, her green face reappeared. She looked at Mave, puzzled, then took her arm. *Come*, Mave heard.

"I can't," Mave said, panic making her forget to moisovo. Her breathing was shallow and tight.

Tear put her palms on Mave's throat then laced her fingers around Mave's neck, the tips touching in the back. Something cool flowed up Mave's neck and down her spine. Slowly the fear and panic washed away, and the clawing sense of suffocation dissolved. Mave's shoulders relaxed, and she could smell the warm night, the smoky cave, and Tear's rock-like scent. She took Mave's hand and led her in.

Their path slanted down, and after a few yards the temperature dropped. Holding Tear's hand, Mave followed her into the darkness. Mave remembered her fear of dark places, but she was separate from it, as though it were locked up.

They turned a corner and far ahead of them a fire glowed. Mave's feet were damp, and she could smell wetness and, faintly, lime.

They neared the fire. Figures crowded around it. Tear and Mave stepped closer to it, and she counted almost fifty, all half-and-halfs. The cave room was large and low-ceilinged.

Tear led Mave to a place in front of the fire, and the others made room for them as they sat down. It was hard to tell the half-and-halfs apart. They all dressed in the same chalky-colored shirts and trousers and had the same short, spiky hair. Mave felt a buzzing in her head, as though she were picking up on the thoughts in everyone's head.

Tear brushed Mave's hand to get her attention.

Careful. You're taking in too much. You'll drown.

How do I turn it off?

Pretend your head is a house. Close off all the rooms but one.

Mave closed her eyes and imagined doors shutting in her head, leaving a small red one opened at the front.

Tear smiled. *My door is red too.*

A commotion sounded at the front of the cave. With the half-and-halfs, she turned to watch someone who stood heads above them walking toward them in the dim light.

"Mave," he said as he neared her, his voice sounding odd in the room where the only noise was the crackling of the fire. It was Beatt, the man who had visited her mother, the man with the warnings and the hump around his middle.

Even in the faint light of the cave, his hump was visible under his cape. He strode toward Mave, his buskins covered in the fine dust from the roads, his cape flapping open. His knees glinted in the firelight. Mave looked at Tear, who smiled at her.

He's a… Tear began but was cut off by Beatt's voice.

"Mave," he said, kneeling next to her.

She could not take her eyes off his knees. Iridescent as pearls and layered like a bird's feathers, scales covered his knees.

He put his finger under Mave's chin and lifted her head. "We must go."

"No," Mave said. She reached for Tear's hand and found nothing beside her but empty space.

You're called, Tear said in her head. *Your turn.*

Mave looked around the room for Tear, into the fifty similar, semi-divine faces staring back at her.

"We need you now," Beatt said.

Hearing the noise of his voice and her own, Mave's connection to the warm, dark world weakened and remembrance of what was happening outside flooded back. With a pang, she remembered Anta and her sisters, the people in the village, her mother, then Turnip and the Executrix. And the white giants.

"There's nothing I can do," Mave said, her voice rising to a cry. "I went to the village. I ran away."

The half-and-halfs shrank away from Mave's cries and the fire, into the gloom behind Mave and Be. In their place, all Mave's old fears gathered around her.

Beatt sat down beside Mave, covering his knees with his cape. "Your mother called them 'pale boys'," he said, looking at his feet. "If only it were so. Do you know what I'm talking about?"

He put his hand on Mave's. It looked like a human hand, except for the thick, horny nails that grew to points. His hand felt warm, and after a moment the heat increased. Then scenes began to appear in Mave's head, of the Executrix and the Gigante, multitudes of them, far outnumbering the villagers, standing near the outskirts of the village. The Executrix and the leader looked down at the village then up at hieros house. Then they dispersed, a small group towards hieros house, a larger group into the town, a few toward the open field where the horses grazed. She saw three and four gather around those people sleeping on the ground, and the rest go in small groups into each of the houses. Several posted themselves at points around the outer circle of buildings.

The people on the ground began to stretch, the sign that they were nearly around the last bend on their trek back from the other side. It was a vulnerable time of their journey.

One of the white giants spied the man in the doorway and strode over and kicked him. The man struggled to all fours, shaking his head. The white giant kicked him again. He fell to his side and tried to crawl away. The white giant laughed and gathered him up as though he were an old blanket and tossed him over his shoulder. He didn't move again.

Another white giant, the leader, shouted at the one who threw the man. He motioned for him to join him. Most of the people were awake now, though still dazed and sleepy. The white giants had roused everyone, dragging them from their houses, hauling them to their feet from where they lay on the ground. The white giants placed them in a long line, stretching from the knoll to outside the village and snaking up the hill to hieros house. Dia's people formed a human chain, each linked by rope that threaded through cuffs on their wrists.

Two white giants stood in the open field beyond the village, trying to catch one of the horses. Like Oats and Wonder, these horses had a shelter but ran free, and would come at a kind word. These men did not know such a basic thing. Instead, they shouted and threw rope looped at the end until they caught one of the horses, its muscles rigid with fear and surprise, its eyes rolling back in its head, rearing repeatedly to break free.

After a time, every living thing in Mave's village was either roped or chained. Their heads were bowed, and they stood still as though in a trance. All raised their heads when the women of hieros house were led from the sleeping building. Their tunics were torn and their faces were bruised. The white giants pushed them into a circle, their backs to the inside of the circle, and tied them tight with rope as though they were a bunch of carrots. Anta raised her bruised face, calling out the sacred words of Ssha magic. One of the white giants struck her down with his fist.

A cry went up then, as the people woke to what had happened.

"No more," Mave said, and the pictures stopped. Anger rose in her, at Tear and at Beatt. "You brought me here while the Gigante were ransacking Dia," she said, speaking through tears. "You did something to do me so I wouldn't sense it. You should have let me be taken with them."

Beatt shook his head in the red glow of the fire, casting his shadow on the dark walls. The half-and-halfs had disappeared into the far reaches of the cave, and Mave's connection with Tear felt broken as though she had dreamed her. "We needed your particular talents."

"My talents?" Mave asked, laughing through her tears. "I have nothing to compare to Ssha magic. I'm afraid of everything."

"Ssha magic can't fight forces like thunderstorms. In Ssha way, thunderstorms aren't meant to be fought; they're meant to run their course. Only this thunderstorm, in the form of the white giants, doesn't want to run its course. It wants to live forever and conquer everything in its path." He opened his palms in a gesture of helplessness. "We have nothing to fight against that."

"Neither do I," Mave said, turning away as hot tears ran down her face.

"Ah, but you do. Your clay chips. You can help us make Ssha

magic safe. We can't fight these invaders, so we must make Ssha knowledge safe. May I see them?"

Mave untied the bag from her belt and handed it to him. She hid her face in her arms, feeling tired, empty, and raw.

Beatt loosened the bag and held up one of the chips. "The knowledge disguised. Hidden yet visible."

Mave raised her head and shook it, suddenly tired and feeling that nothing was comprehensible. "They're just pictures I like to draw when…." She stopped herself. Even now, at the end of the world, it might not do to confess to breaking the rules.

Beatt smiled. "When you talk with the Ssha? It's all right, Mave. They've been talking with you for a long time. You were the only one quiet enough and awake enough in your village for them to talk with."

Mave thought how her fears had increased as she'd gotten older, and suddenly it made sense. The closer her future had come, the more she had wanted to hide.

"What do you want me to do?"

"The knowledge must be kept alive. We'll need it in the coming times. What if the knowledge were broken down and each piece of it assigned a symbol, something that stood for it? So that if one knew how, pieced together with each other, the symbols formed a whole."

"But my symbols are just the different phases of the moon and astrological wheels."

"You must go deeper into the caves. You must meet with the Ssha. They'll communicate the knowledge and symbols to you, and you'll commit them to memory, then to clay chips."

"Deeper into the caves?" Mave's stomach turned at the thought of deeper, darker places.

"The Ssha are a half-day's ride from here, out of the foothills and into the mountains proper."

"Why can't a half-and-half do it? They're your decipherers."

Beatt shook his head. "They've tried. Half-and-halfs can decipher what's given to them but can't abstract the information into a symbol."

"Then you. You're smart. You can move in both worlds. You should be able to do it."

"No, Mave. Maybe later there will be more like you. But right now, there's only you."

She jumped up. "I have to see my mother first. I have to find out what she would say. She'd know."

Beatt looked sadly at the packed dirt of the cave floor. "If you want to see your mother, hold my hand, and I'll show you your mother." He paused and met Mave's gaze. "Your mother, my half-sister," he added.

"Your what?" Mave said.

"One of the Ssha chose one of your people as their mate, not just as a human to breed with, as was done with the women of hieros house: your grandmother."

Mave's head reeled—with Gramia? Like Mave's mother, she'd been star counsel, and she died when Mave was very young, but mostly Mave remembered a sweet old woman who lost her memory in the end. She had died in her sleep. Then it clicked. That's why Beatt looked familiar. She had seen him at Gramia's crossing over ceremony. He nodded as the details flooded her mind. "You wore all yellow," Mave said, "and carried lilacs."

"You couldn't have been more than two. You have an amazing memory, Mave. And that is yet another reason why you can help the Ssha."

Beatt crossed to Mave and took her hands in his. As he did, a current coursed through Mave and it hit her. This half man, half lizard was her uncle. She was related to the Ssha.

"Everything's in place," he said. "Your ability to moisovo, your talent with the chips, and the way you've taught yourself to shift your spirit into other forms."

He smiled at the look on Mave's face. "The Ssha miss very little. Please, Mave, will you do it? Will you help the Ssha?"

She thought of her mother. To her, administrator extraordinaire, a task was a task, and if it involved danger, so much the better, for then you could prove your mettle. Perhaps Mave could prove to Audria that she had it in her to be the kind of daughter she wanted. But then it occurred to Mave she wasn't sure she still had a mother.

"Show me my mother," Mave said. "If she's alive, I'll do it."

"Take my hand," Beatt said.

Mave put her hand in his, warm, dry, rough, and the familiar rise of heat began. Her head swam with images then settled down to a scene picturing the side of her house. Then the view switched to inside the walls, into her secret hiding place. There, her mother sat crouched, like a cat ready to pounce. Her hair had come loose and billowed in a cloud of black curl. Her eyes were on fire, and she grinned like a goblin. She started as the ground shook with approaching horses, then sneered as the hooves pounded into our yard. "Come on, come on," she seemed to be saying.

Mother, implored Mave in her mind. Her mother cocked her head briefly, as though she heard Mave, then smiled slyly and pushed the brick that opened a small section of wall. With a wave, she crawled out then leaped beyond Mave's sight.

She was alive, but for how long with her foolish ways? "I've seen enough," Mave said. "I'll do it. Let's go."

Beatt and Mave rose from where they sat at the fire. She glanced back at the half-and-halfs, who now sat gathered in a far corner of the cave with their heads bowed.

Tear, Mave sent her name out, *are you there? Will you say goodbye to me?*

The silence in her head was the only answer.

She followed Beatt to the slender tunnel that would lead them out. He strode into the darkness, and as Mave stepped forward, the old panic overtook her, flooding her. The walls began to close in on her, and screams fought their way out of her throat. Just as they began to erupt, she felt a pressure on her neck and the cool streams of relief like Tear had given her before. Wherever she was, Tear was sending help.

"Mave," Beatt called from farther down the tunnel.

"I'm coming," she called and turned back to face the darkness and walk blindly into it.

It didn't take long before she had joined Beatt at the mossy mouth of the entrance. It was night, the eastern sky as dark as the walls of the cave, the final quarter moon a slice of light.

5
The Ways of the Wise Reptiles

BEATT PEERED OUT INTO THE dark. "Can you call the horses?"

Mave whistled a trilling sound and below them, where the foothills leveled off and became grassier, large bodies shifted in the brush then sounded the thump of hooves. The horses approached.

Oats came to Mave in the darkness, nuzzling her neck. As Mave rested her head against Oats' neck, Mave tried again to send words out to Tear. *Tear, are you there?* Mave looked at the dark shape of her Uncle Beatt patting Wonder and whispering in her ear. Could he hear her every thought? Mave knew how to moisovo but didn't know how it worked.

"I'll tell you," Beatt said, turning and stepping closer to her.

She jumped, startled. "I don't think I care for you being so present in my head."

In the dark he looked handsome in a reptilian sort of way, his long tail of hair slung over his shoulder. "My apologies," he said, with a slight bow of his head.

Mave turned back to give Oats a brisk rub. "But you can still tell me how it works."

"It's like throwing a ball down a path with thick brambles so no one else can hear or see the ball, except the person on the other end. But even then, they must know to check the path for incoming balls, be aware they may be there. Do you see?"

"I hadn't pictured it as purposeful as that," Mave said. She had thought of it more as a bee finding its way to honey, a lazy, weaving stream of thoughts finding its way to the object of desire. It felt that way when the Ssha's thoughts entered her head, and even more so when Tear's had.

"When you're first learning," Beatt said, "it's like this." He slowly drew a zig-zag in the air from his head to Mave's. "You should watch baby half-and-halfs when they're just learning. The air becomes heavy, like the water of a swollen river."

"Yes," Mave said, impatient for the discussion to be over. She didn't see, but didn't want him to think her stupid, and she was anxious to get this trip underway. She was tired and starting to have second thoughts. What if she embarrassed herself by wavering, or worse, crying? It was getting harder to keep pushing back her thoughts, and her fears, about what was happening in her town.

"We'll talk more later," Beatt said, stepping back into darkness to climb on Wonder's back. "It's time to go."

They rode deeper into the foothills as the moon slowly dropped out of sight. Wonder and Oats were as sure-footed as goats and picked a path through the hills as they rose into mountains. Mave grew sleepy as they rode higher. It felt as though they had left the earth and were ascending a trail of stars into heaven.

Just as her eyes began to droop in sleep, the sky far to the east, in the direction of Dia, was torn apart by a hurl of light.

The horses did not buck, as Mave thought they would, but stopped and became still. She and the horses stared at the exploding sky. The first burst was followed by a red glow, which had to be flames.

Mave peered at Beatt. She tried to feel his presence. At first she felt nothing, then it came to her, as though she were smelling or hearing something, only she was feeling it—the burning smells and the wails of people. Beatt's emotions flowed through her, his shock, his sorrow, his dismay, and a recognition in him, as though he were thinking, "so that's what it meant."

Mave sensed his shoulders slumping forward, as though heavy with weight. "What is it?" she asked, her voice timid from the fear of being wrong or stupid.

"Nephthar," came his muffled voice in the darkness.

That was the word from the half-and-half's dreams and the white giant to the Executrix. "Naphtha," Mave said, pronouncing it as the Gigante had.

"Not purification," he said. "Fire. Not fire that warms but fire that explodes." He paused. "They have a weapon that kills many more people than a lance or a club."

"What do they make it from?"

"Their dried hunks of earth. Peat. When very dry it distills to an oily liquid. A few drops on the peat, and with one touch of fire, it explodes."

All the life seemed to have gone out of him. "With their naphtha, they can take whatever they want."

Even when the wise reptiles lived among Mave's people during her grandmother's time, as legend said they once did, there was no inkling of such a people.

"If they're that powerful," said Be, "I'm not sure our magic can hold against them. Our magic has kept peace for many thousands of years."

Mave thought of Turnip and how he had paid as a victim of keeping that peace.

She started crying. She felt like an idiot but couldn't help herself. This was all too much, and she was tired and now she was scared.

Beatt's hand reached out in the darkness and rested on her shoulder. "I'm sorry, I forget that you are young. With your silence and serious questions, you have the bearing of someone much older. You're tired. Do you want to ride with me? Oats will follow, and you can sleep."

Mave shook her head, though of course Beatt couldn't see her. "I'll sleep on Oats. She won't let me fall." She lay down on Oats, wrapping her arms around Oats' neck, her legs dangling off her sides, and fell asleep.

When Mave woke, the sun was just rising. She lay in a thicket of brambly bushes. Beatt had laid his purple cape over her, and the rising sun glinted off gold threads woven into it. Drowsily, she picked at these, the sun warm on her fingers. She could hear Beatt outside the thicket, humming.

I'm lighting, came the words, *not humming*.

Mave was awake now. The reception of his words had buzzed her awake. She threw off Beatt's cape and realized if he was not wearing his cape, what was he wearing?

She crawled to an opening in the bushes and peered out. She gasped. The sun rose in a blaze over the top of the horizon, and Beatt stood facing it, his arms spread wide as though ready to catch it. He wore a simple shirt similar to Tear's and leather buskins, out of which rose his legs, green and scaled and iridescent in the sunlight. A magnificent tail flicked behind him. Half man, half lizard, Beatt greeted the sun with open arms and a humming sound in his throat.

For a few moments, he seemed unaware of Mave's focus on him. Then the sun crested the horizon, and the spell was broken. He dropped his arms, turned to her, and smiled.

"You'll learn to do this too, taking in the light, storing up for when you go underground."

She stood, feeling foolish, and gaped. He was like a centaur in his perfect division of man and animal.

Beatt laughed. "I'm a good introduction to our people, no? You can get used to us in stages—first the half-and-halfs, then me, then those who are all lizard from head to toe."

She was beginning to see the resemblance between Beatt and her mother. They bounced back. Beatt's people were on the brink of extinction, the Gigante had overrun Dia, and still he could rise and light with the sun and laugh.

They ate a meal of burdock root from a patch Mave found, skinning away the bitter brown skin and crunching the sweet white root. Soon they moved farther up into the hills. Beatt had retrieved his cape and swung it around his shoulders, this time letting his tail swing loose. He saw Mave looking. "I'm safe this far up into the hills. The Gigante's horses are ill-trained to navigate these rocky hills. They'd panic at the slippery footholds and would buck at the Gigante's uncertainty."

The thick brambles rose in a low-ceilinged canopy over the narrow path.

They traveled this way for some time, until the sun began to set. They reached a clearing where the canopy remained but the close borders of brambles opened up into a wide circle. Up ahead, the path abruptly grew narrow again, like the neck of a bottle. Be stopped and swung off Wonder. Mave did the same and began rooting around in the undergrowth for their next meal.

"No," he said, "You and I won't share a meal for some time."

"Why not?" Mave asked.

"This is where I must leave, and you must go on alone."

"Alone?"

"You see that path?" he said, pointing to the bottleneck. "You see how it's no taller or wider than you? Like it's a perfect fit? Well, that's exactly what it is. If I was supposed to accompany you, the path would be big enough for me, too. They—my wise reptilian cousins in the caves—decide who will come and who won't."

"You mean they send someone out here with a blade to carve a path?"

Beatt laughed. "No, they can accomplish all of it without moving from their caves."

"If they're so powerful, why don't they stop the Gigante?"

Beatt's smile faded. "Our magic is only as strong as the believers behind it. Up here, it's easy. Below, the invaders are changing beliefs through fear and coercion."

"Then get the Gigante up here."

Be sighed. "You make it sound so easy. What would lure them up here?"

She threw her hands up, exasperated that he could not see the obvious. "The Ssha. The source of peace and the mysteries of the void. The Goddess. Lure the Gigante with the chance to get rid of their enemy."

Beatt looked shaken. "We couldn't risk that. Come on, now, the sun's about to set, and you must be on your way."

Mave turned to the setting sun and spread her arms wide as she had seen Be do, storing up light.

"No," Beatt said sharply, grabbing Mave's arms and spinning her toward him. "Never light from the setting sun, no matter how brilliant its rays."

Her cheeks burned in embarrassment at his scolding. Too

humiliated to speak, and her eyes filled up with tears.

His voice softened. "The setting sun is the dying sun. Only once in a person's life does she light with the dying sun, and I hope that your transition is far off for you."

The sun dropped behind the hills, leaving them in a dusky light. "It is, however, your time to go down the path. Quickly now." He gave her a gentle push toward the path, which, as she peered at it in the dim light, seemed to be growing narrower. "Hurry," Beatt said, starting to run and pulling Mave with him onto the path.

"But," Mave said, panting, "how will I know where to go? Or what to do?" A rumbling started, like roots growing rapidly out of the ground. "How will I find the caves?"

Beatt shouted over the thunderous rumbling. "The same way you knew how to carry on those conversations with us and the way you heard the cries of the people who had been bombed, too far away to hear with the human ear. In you go." He pushed her through the opening, now no bigger than a hieros house shield, and called out, "The luck of the void to you."

And then he was gone, as was everything in that world, as behind Mave the opening grew over with thorns and brambles and was quickly a solid wall.

6
Little Pictures on Clay Chips

THERE WAS NO LIGHT. IT was solid darkness. Mave lifted her arms and touched the sides of the cave, which felt like cool, dry rock. She lost her sense of direction and turned several times. She took two steps and banged into the back wall, what had been the opening and now was solid rock. Crossing hand over hand, she turned herself in the opposite direction and began a shuffling walk forward.

She walked and walked. Time ceased to have meaning, and even the substance of her memories was annulled, as though they had gone from three-dimensional pictures in her mind to drawings in the dirt. That should have made her cry, for they were her best memories of Anta and even her mother in her better moments. All of it slid away, as though Mave's memories were being sanded off her brain.

A rasping sounded somewhere around her, a wheezing hum that rose and fell. Then she could hear that it was really like a breath, an inhale and an exhale, but sounded like a papery hiss.

Slowly she began to perceive a light, a glow, far, far down the cave tunnel, still with the hissing breath coming from somewhere. It surrounded her the way a mother's heartbeat surrounds the child in her womb. Mave shuffled toward the light, then, as the light grew brighter and she could see where she was going, she began to run, her sandals slapping on the stone floor.

As she ran, the hissing breath grew louder and louder and was no longer gentle but growing and insistent, like a swarm of bees. Mave stopped abruptly, near panic. The light was so close, but how could she protect herself from whatever made the sound? She started running again—she had to get out of this darkness and into the light—and, after puffing out her chest with breath, she swung her arms wildly about her head, protection from the imagined bees, and started yelling as loudly as she could.

She ran as hard and wild and loudly as she could, and so it was a shock when in one sudden moment she was in the light and had slammed against a wall. She was at the end of the tunnel, and in the light. Eyes, many eyes, stared as the hissing breath revealed its source. She stood there, rubbing her elbows, dazed from her slam against the wall, out of breath from her run.

A fire burned in the center of a round room. Mave's eyes adjusted. Seven giant lizards, the Ssha, sat in a semi-circle behind the fire, watching her, breathing loudly in and out in a communal, hissing breath.

Uncle Beatt was one thing, thought Mave, *these giant lizards another*.

One spoke in a voice croaky as though unused. "Your people have changed since our time with you. Is that your new method of locomotion?"

Mave opened her mouth to speak, but nothing came out.

Steam rose off their backs. Mave stared at them, unable to

speak. Their heads were crested with a tiara of triangular points. Her head was awash with voices, words and fragments, as though a whole town had crowded inside. It was all too much. She sank to her knees and held her head in her hands.

She heard or felt the words, "To her," and it was as though a presence rose out of each Ssha's head, passed through the fire and came to rest in a close circle around her. Mave's eyes were closed during all of this, so she apprehended it all by feel, as Beatt had described to her, tried to teach her.

When she could speak again, she raised her head. The Ssha still sat as motionless as before on the other side of the fire, which had burned down to glowing embers, but somehow they didn't look as threatening.

"Show us your stones," one of them said, but Mave couldn't tell which, for no one's mouth moved.

Am I starting to get it? she thought. *Am I actually hearing their unspoken words in my head?*

Yes, you are, came another voice, that of the first who had spoken. *It's much easier for us this way. At one time we used words when we lived among your people, but even then it was a mix of words and mind-verse. Too, it is more powerful than speech. Mind-verse can go anywhere, to any time.*

Mave listened and relaxed. Her gaze drifted upward. The ceiling of the cave had spikes of frosty rock hanging down, and the eyes of the Ssha, who even sitting down rose to six feet, were focused on a point behind her on the wall. She turned and saw what appeared to be a giant collar hanging on a peg just above her head.

What is that? she asked, turning back to face the Ssha. She sensed a guarded hesitancy. Then the words came. *It's the Scale of Truth. It represents that which we come from and will return to.* The tone changed abruptly as another voice cut in. *Show us your stones now.*

This one seemed tenser than the others. *Yes*, went another voice, sounding resigned, as though giving in.

Mave felt in her pocket for her bag of clay chips. She took it out, shook the chips into her hand, and showed the Ssha. None of the Ssha moved. Mave slowly walked around the fire to stand directly in front of the Ssha. They smelled like the white lime that served as mortar between bricks when mixed with water. Their entire bodies were scaled and ridged. Sitting, they rose taller than her. One took the chip with her claw, examined it, and then passed it along.

This will do, Mave heard in her head, from the tense one, she thought.

Now we must prepare you for absorption of our ideas, our magic, all that you must find a symbol or picture for.

In one motion they all rose, towering over Mave. Her knees began to shake. *Prepare me?* she thought. She had visions of being tied up, trussed like a chicken bound for the oven. She held back as the Ssha shuffled slowly into the next room, where another fire flickered. Was it too late to escape?

She jumped as the remaining Ssha put her claw on her shoulder. Mave felt kindness in her touch, distant but gentle. Slowly, Mave turned to face her.

Mave's eyes were level with the Ssha's scaled belly. Mave tilted back her head and raised her eyes to the reptile's, slow-blinking slits. The Ssha knelt on one knee.

"Take this," she said in a croaky voice, abandoning mind-verse, and handing Mave a small bowl of white liquid.

Mave hesitated. It was too late to go back, but she was afraid of what lay ahead, and this white liquid appeared to be the first step toward that uncertain future.

"Think of it as a bridge between our minds and yours," she

said, still using her physical voice.

To Mave's ears, the Ssha's voice sounded out of place in this shadowy cave, where it seemed as though the true power lay in the vibrations behind words and sounds.

"That is so," her lizard friend said, reading her mind, "but I thought you wouldn't be as scared if I spoke to you as one of your people might."

Mave nodded and remained still for a moment, letting the vibrations settle in her. The lizard nodded as Mave did this, seeming to understand and approve. When Mave's insides had come to rest, she let her gut speak. She took the bowl and drank down its contents.

Nothing seemed to be happening as Mave followed the lizard into the adjoining room, which was dark as a mother's womb. The vibrations she'd been feeling came together, like strands weaving themselves into a braid. Once joined, a rhythmic pulsing began, like a drum beat but not, and she sensed all the Ssha forming a circle. They began a shuffling dance. One of them plucked at Mave's sleeve and drew her into the circle.

The soundless vibrations grew in intensity until her bones shook with their pounding. Her arms lost definition first, then her legs and feet. Where they had been a solid thing they broke up into bits which grew ever smaller until they were dots. As her body was obliterated, so too was her apprehension of it and her ability to touch, see, and hear. Her sense of self went next, dissolving like powder into water. The "I" of Mave was no longer. "Mave" was the floor of the cave, her sister and brother lizards' toes. She was a thread in a giant veil of cloth. She had fallen to the bottom of the well of reality. Pictures flooded her head. Scenes of a man and a lizard fighting it out over a mound of grass covered with strange gypsum markings. Of a whole town of people floating in the sky in a giant bowl with a lid; of making a meal out of the moon.

You are Mavealeph, sister to the Ssha, Sister Aleph, Mave heard in her head, just before she lost consciousness.

☾

Many hours later she woke. The fires burned low. There was complete silence. No hissing breath, and no sense of anyone or any presence. She sat up. She had been sleeping in a nest of dried grasses on the stone floor. Her trousers, shirt and jacket reeked of wood smoke and dampness. There hadn't been time to pack any extra clothing. Unless the Ssha kept spare shifts for the random young woman who visited their caves, she would be smelling these scents for some time. She felt hollow and light. She looked around. No one was there. All the wise reptiles were gone. A snuffling snore made her jump. What had the Ssha left behind?

She slowly rose and crept toward the heap that was making the noise. All at once it threw back its cloak. It was Beatt.

"Beatt," Mave said, throwing herself into his arms. "How did you get in here?"

"The usual way," he said, pointing. When Mave looked she saw that it was the mouth of the cave. The sun was just rising. She looked expectantly at him, and he nodded. They both rose and together stood at the mouth of the cave and lighted, like two candles, igniting themselves with the light of the rising sun. A sense of rightness came over Mave as she fitted herself into this new rhythm.

When they were done, they sat at the mouth of the cave, and Beatt gave Mave fruit from the pockets of his cloak. She realized she had not eaten since last night. She felt dazed.

She shook her head. "Be, what happened last night?"

He turned and looked at Mave with a worried look on his face.

"Last night? You've been here three days. Don't you remember anything?"

Mave shook her head. "Just that I danced with the Ssha."

Beatt rose and pointed to the corner. "You've been working."

She went to the corner. Ten clay chips were laid out in two rows. Each had a design or picture etched in gypsum. She looked at one closely. It told a mini story. She turned to Be, unable to comprehend. "I did this?"

He nodded. "After the dancing, the reptiles went deeper into the caves. There's a whole labyrinth below us. Their magic is safe now. Thank you, Mave."

Mave couldn't take it all in. She had drunk the white liquid, danced like a wild girl, then—she remembered now—had her head filled with a host of strange images and pictures. She remembered losing her sense of self, as though she'd been swallowed up in a tankard of ale. There her memory left off. She had painted these pictures on these clay chips, drawing on the pool of images into which she'd fallen.

On the first chip, a flower with layers of petals bloomed out of a full moon, a symbol of the Great Mother, her earthly and heavenly powers, and her mysteries. The next, two Ssha fingers, scaled and clawed, rose out of the dirt, like spring shoots, showing that all life comes from nothing. The third showed a dancing rabbit, the marshalling of silly energy that sometimes is the only approach to life. On the fourth was drawn the same rabbit, only dead and staked form the four corners, while a bony woman, heavy with child, stood ready with her knife to skin him for dinner, symbolizing the sacrifice of energies required for continued life.

The remaining six were a mystery to Mave. One seemed to change depending on what angle she held it up to the light, its image shifting like swirling sand. It was warmer to the touch than the others. Another showed a man with a painted face and a feathered headdress guarding a melting heart. The seventh pictured oblongs of various heights rising off the horizon with stick figures of people standing inside. The oblongs crowded the horizon, leaving no room for flowers or trees. At the very bottom of this chip, a Ssha lay on her back as though buried, yet extended a clawed hand toward the people in the oblongs. On the ninth Mave had drawn three women in gowns standing on a dais in front of hundreds of stick figures representing people crowded off to the sides. This wouldn't be so strange except that behind the women shone two suns, implying a land far different from Mave's. The tenth and final chip again showed hundreds of stick figures except that most were piled up as though dead. A few appeared to rise, as though the sky were drawing them up, all heading toward the corner where there was a circle with two suns, and Mave guessed this represented the home of the three goddesses shown on the ninth chip.

"We can't stay," Beatt said, taking Mave's shoulders. "It's time to return to the world, which sorely needs the Ssha's magic in the form of your chips."

"Have you seen my mother while I was here?" she asked.

"No," Beatt said, abruptly. "That's why we must go. Mave, I don't want to scare you, but one of the half-and-halfs keeps having the same dream: a column of gold light rises out of the night sky and blots out Venus and the full moon."

Her heart beat faster. "Was it Tear who dreamed it?"

He shook his head. "The Ssha asked Tear to go the next level, deeper inside Ssha Mountain, and remain there as a conduit between the Ssha and the first level of half-and-halfs. We've not heard from her and probably won't. To be a conduit, she must stay still and empty herself of who she was. The half-and-half who had the dream was Stel, one close to Tear."

Maybe it is the half-and-half way to leave so abruptly, Mave thought, *but I don't like it.* Tear had easily forged a bond with Mave then just as easily left the above-earth and Mave without a word. She made her heart grow cold to bear the pain. Be looked at her, concerned. She spoke before he could.

"We must go now. We must hurry." Mave swept the chips up into her shirt pocket. "Let's go."

"Here." He handed Mave a drawstring sack made of seasoned barka leaves which resembled hide. "The reptiles' gift to you. It's for the chips. You can carry them in it."

Mave dropped them in one by one. "Alright, then, let's go."

Back they went, riding Oats and Wonder through the craggy black mountains, past the tangled brush that lead into the foothills. Mave was going home.

"Is that fog?" Mave asked Beatt, pointing to what looked like low clouds covering her village below.

Beatt would not look at Mave. He looked away, then down. "I should have told you at the cave."

Mave rode up to him and shook his arm.

"Be, what is it?"

He raised his head. His eyes were full of tears. "That is smoke from the fires the Gigante set when they took the villagers and ransacked their homes."

Mave's throat constricted as though a rope tightened about her neck. "My mother?" she whispered.

Beatt looked away. Tears spilled out of his eyes and down his cheeks. "No one knows. She was last seen holding a Gigante's head under water in a pig's drinking trough."

Mave laughed while at the same time a gulping sob overtook her. *My mother*, she thought. She'd thought little of her during her time in the Ssha's cave, but then she rarely thought of her. Her mother was always there, like the sun in the morning and the moon at night, and who thinks of those things much during the day, except to say the sun is bright or what a beautiful moon? And, too, they had so often not gotten along. When Mave thought of someone kind and comforting, she thought of Anta, not her mother.

Sometimes, when Mave had sat in her hiding place behind the chimney, escaping there after her mother had made fun of her paintings, she played a game with herself: Who dies first? If someone had to die first, her mother or Anta, who would she choose? It was always her mother.

She began to cry. Beatt bowed his head. It was not the Ssha way to comfort the grieving. *How do I know this?* thought Mave. It must have been one of the things she learned in the caves and the knowledge was coming to the surface. In the Ssha way, grief was honored and allowed to go its course. To stop it or change it into mere sadness was a sin, because it was through grief that transformation of the soul took place. To interrupt it with a hug or kind word would be like interrupting a supernova as the star explodes to become a hundred million new things. She had never felt such power as this knowledge and strong emotion course through her, like two rushing rivers guided by the earth's movement.

There was nothing to do but go forward, down Ssha Mountain and into what was left of her village. At the base of the mountain, Beatt wrapped his tail around his waist, binding it with a large strip of cloth. A tremor went through her, like a rabbit who sensed a storm coming.

Instead of his purple cape, Beatt pulled on a loose tunic of ash-smeared sackcloth. With a sharp rock he tore holes in his leggings, then with the same rock beat his leather buskins until they looked as though an animal had chewed them up and spit them out.

He looked up as Mave stared. "We can't travel looking like we've escaped the fighting, which we have. We'd be easy targets. We need to look as beaten as everyone else." He handed Mave a sackcloth and the sharp rock, and soon she looked like him, stained and crumpled.

"The final touch," he said, taking up the sharp rock again and laying his head down on another flat rock, then began to saw at his beautiful hair until he was left with ragged locks that hung to his ears. The only recognizable thing left about him was his eyes and their diamond pupils. Even his nose, a bare rise off his face, allowing only enough room for two narrow nostrils, was hidden behind grime.

"You're next," he said.

"But my hair's already short."

"That's the problem. You're too clearly aligned with hieros house. With what was hieros house. Non-hieros house women under the Gigante cover the shame of their short hair with scarves."

Mave stared at him. "Shame?" she said, uncomprehending.

"Not my words," he said. "Theirs." He glanced at the late afternoon sun, still high in the summer sky. "We have some time, but not much. The Gigante allow no one in Dia out after dark."

Again, his words were almost too much for Mave to take in or understand. She could only parrot them back in disbelief. "No one after dark? How does anyone walk the borderlands?"

Beatt sighed. "They don't, Mave. No one does."

Mave sat down on the ground. "How do the Gigante stop them?"

Beatt sat down beside her. "For the moment, the invaders are keeping the people of your village in an encampment not far from the town. The people in the encampment are guarded. Only a few have recovered from being awakened before they were fully returned from the borderlands. The Gigante allow the men in that group to go back to what's left of the village to scrounge for anything valuable to bring back to the invaders. Most of the people, though, are lost spirits."

"Give me your rock," Mave said, and with it she hacked and pounded his cape until she had a square of battered purple cloth. She placed the piece of cloth over her head, draping it so it nearly covered all her face.

"There is one more thing," Beatt said, and bit his lip. "With the Gigante having conquered Dia, we must look like a conquered people in all respects." He looked away. "You'd be suspect as a free girl. You'd be less suspect if you were considered my property."

And so they rode into Dia, Beatt leading her horse, Mave's head shrouded and bowed, her hands bound.

7
Sign of the Crone, Traveler Rising

IT WAS A FINE SUMMER evening. The setting sun turned the sky pink and gold, and the winds were still, but only in the heavens was anything all right. What had once been a village was now charred stumps of debris. A blackened door was the only thing left standing at one house. All around it the rest of the house lay burned.

A few people were about, all men, no one Mave recognized. They appeared to be going through the rubble, perhaps looking for anything of value. They did it with very little energy, like children who've been told to do something they didn't want to. They glanced at Mave and Be, then went back to their work.

At the edge of town, Beatt and Mave paused. The horses bowed their heads, as though they too felt the weight of what had happened.

"Do you want to go on?" Beatt asked.

Mave nodded. They took their time getting to her house, as

though Beatt, Mave and the horses were out for a leisurely stroll.

Too soon, they were at her home. Or what was left of it. Beatt and Mave sat on their horses and stared. The stable and the house were piles of rubble and ash. The piles rose high, nearly as tall as a person.

There was nothing left of Mave's old life. She was numb. She felt blown apart and hollowed out, as empty and cavernous as a skeleton's ribcage. She stared, feeling Beatt's presence. He too had lost much—his half-sister, and his own people to the intolerance of a time. Mave imagined a future when it would be safe for the giant reptiles to live again on the surface. Would there ever be such a time again?

A figure crouched at the far end of the burned ruins of their house. It looked like an old woman picking among the ashes, bent with her head covered in dirty brown cloth.

"Be, look, someone's there. Maybe it's someone I know from the village."

"It seems unlikely," he said. "I thought the invaders didn't leave any women free." He looked off into the distant hills, toward Ssha Mountain. "I'm tired. You go see who it is."

"Trussed up as I am?"

He loosened the rope just enough so that Mave could manage her horse's reins but not so much that she would appear free.

"Be quick," he said. "The sun's almost set, and we can't be caught out after dark."

Oats picked her way through the cold ashes and crumbs of Mave's house. To her surprise her mother flooded her mind, her smells of hemp and smoky sweet grass and her big voice calling her. For a woman who often seemed too busy for her daughter, she spent a lot of time calling Mave to her. She was so present and real in Mave's mind, it was almost as though she were right there with her.

The old woman ignored her and picked away at the piles of ashes.

"Hello," Mave called. "I'm Mave, star counsel's daughter." She rode up awkwardly with her semi-bound hands.

"Shut yer trap," the hunched figure snarled.

The essence of Mave's mother rose up so strongly it was like running into a wall of flame.

Is this grief? thought Mave. Would it lessen once she was away from this place?

"Who are you?" she said to the old woman. "You're not from this place." Something chilled her. "I want you to leave," Mave said. "This is not your place."

"Any place is my place," she growled, swaying from the waist as she bent over the ground.

"Mave," Beatt called, "we must go. Now!"

Mave looked off into the distance. Riders on horses barreled toward them. The Gigante were coming.

"Hurry," Beatt cried, galloping toward Mave. "The sun is set. They'll kill us."

The Gigante's horses thundered toward them. The ground shook with their pounding hooves. Beatt's horse, Wonder, reared and screamed, and Beatt lost his hold and fell to the ground.

"Beatt," Mave shrieked as the Gigante closed in on them.

"I can't," he yelled back, as Wonder galloped away, toward Ssha Mountain. "My leg. I think it's broken. Go," he shouted, "go now while you can."

"Not without you." Mave shouted. "If you die, I die."

At this, the crouching old woman sprang toward Beatt and hauled him up and into Mave's saddle. He fainted against Mave in pain as his leg twisted in the effort.

The old woman screamed, "Ride," and smacked Mave's horse on its rump. As she did, her hood fell back to reveal a welcome sight: Audria—her mother.

Mave could not look back as Oats flew over the fields, bearing Beatt and herself to safety. They were not followed, and she knew her mother had distracted the Gigante. If Mave and her mother had not been related, Mave would have been grateful and would have viewed the act as heroic. Instead, Mave's emotions were a mass of warring feelings—confusion, pride, exasperation, and a worrying that pierced her heart like a knife tip. *How could you have done that?* she hissed in her mind to her mother.

The next day, after Beatt and Mave had reached the mouth of the cave deep in the Ssha Mountains and they had bound his broken leg to a sapling and relieved his pain with a paste Mave made out of crushed, purplish-blue skullcap flowers, Beatt cursed himself for not knowing the old woman was Audria.

"If only I'd have sensed her there, we would have had time for all three of us to escape."

They sat near the mouth of the cave, staring out at the gray and drizzly sky.

Mave thought of how flooded she'd been with her but had also not made the connection. "But isn't it obvious she didn't want us to make the connection?" Mave said. "She's as skilled as you when it comes to the power of the mind, what she projects and what others perceive."

Beatt slowly nodded. "Yes, you're right. I should have figured that out. I'm slipping, Mave. I've been too much in the world." He glanced behind into the cave. "I'll have to go back soon."

A burr of panic started up in her stomach. "Go back?" she said.

"I haven't lighted for days," he said dreamily, as though he hadn't heard her, "but that's all right, I'll manage, I'll…"

Beatt drifted off, mumbling to himself, then his chin dropped to his chest.

"Beatt," Mave said sharply and shook his shoulder. Slowly he raised his head and when his eyes met hers she sat back in shock. The iris had spread to cover the whites of his eyes and the pupil, already a diamond of black, had lengthened to a long, thin sliver, like that of a snake.

He turned away and put his head in his hands. "Don't be afraid," he said after a moment, his voice muffled. His head bowed, he sat quietly for a time then slowly raised his head, his eyes returned to normal. "I'm only half human," he said, "and that is the weaker side. My Ssha side will always rise up to claim me, particularly when I've been ignoring it."

The burr began again. Beatt began to feel less tangible to Mave as they sat there, and either he was disappearing or she was sensing a future without him.

"Both." He turned to her and smiled sadly. "I must return to the caves, put on the scale of truth, and sink into all that I am."

Mave plucked at the ragged burlap of her tunic. "What about me?" Her voice was small and choked. This was her version of being like her mother, and it was a pale reflection. But it was all she had as an alternative to breaking down into tears.

Beatt stared straight ahead. "You must go on alone."

The burr of fear turned to anger. "You knew this all along, didn't you? You knew that it all would come to this: my life destroyed."

"Mave, whose isn't?" Beatt said, his head sinking again into his hands.

"You might have told me," she said, her teeth clenched.

"You wouldn't have come. You would have died in the Gigante's first foray into Dia. You would have... Mave, don't."

She had risen to her feet and emptied the bag of clay chips on the cave floor. The chips that held the secrets of Ssha knowledge, preserved for future generations. She took a large flat rock, one good for grinding, and raised it up above those chips, which now symbolized to her loss and sorrow.

At that moment, her physical body seemed to crumble like a dirt clod and while she physically stayed where she was, poised to destroy the only symbols of the reptiles' knowledge, her mind, heart and soul were pulled out of time and space and into another place, where voices crooned like a lullaby. Understanding life, as past, present, and future faded, and there was only a comforting nothing, and the voices, hissing, whispery, papery voices, singing almost but not quite, shushing and hushing. And then, so clearly, her mother's voice, calling her: *Mave? Mave, where are you?*

I'm here, Mave answered. *I'm here. Can you hear me?*

Ah, there you are.

Her voice floated to Mave, a tendril of music making its way to her as though they were underwater, though she had never been in waters quite so deep.

Then her mother laughed. *Do you remember*, she said, *me talking to you this way when you were inside me? Even then you didn't want me to find you. But that's changed, hasn't it?*

Mother, where are you?

It's not yet safe to say. Though the Gigante don't have our skill at mind-verse, they seem to have other ways of spying on us. Have they tapped into mind-verse? Are they listening in on our conversations somehow? We don't know yet. It's really quite interesting, the methods these northerners bring.

Mother, Mave tried to shout with her mind, *when are you coming to get me?*

A silence then, as deep as sorrow.

You're not coming to get me, are you?

No. I'm sorry, Mave. All of us have roles to play, and you, born under the sign of the Crone, Traveler rising, have a role that will be harder than most. You will travel alone but not unaided. You can always reach me in mind-verse. With practice, you can reach the wise reptiles, though that takes a deeper concentration. And when you reach them, you will not hear words; they are so deeply in that even their physical bodies have begun to lose definition, boundaries. They communicate now in slow vibrations, which you must translate into images and then into words. And from time to time, they will call on you to assist the others they pull below. For the uninitiated, it will feel shattering, and the Ssha need you to help those who descend, now and in the future. The Gigante have given birth to themselves and a new era, and we cannot stop it. It must run its course. But the wise lizards will always be here, even if in less tangible form, keeping the old rhythms alive, introducing others to them.

I don't care, Mave said, *I don't care. I want my life back. I want Anta and our house back. I want you back. Mother, please.*

I'm sorry, sweeten, she said. Her voice began to fade.

Don't go, Mave cried. *What do I do next?*

Put down that rock.

And then she was gone, and Mave was back to herself, standing at the mouth of the cave, holding the big rock above her head. Slowly she lowered it and gently set it down.

Beatt was gone. All that remained was a pile of rags, what had been his clothing.

How could she be emptier? Without home, mother, or friend, she faced a world she no longer knew, where she could be killed for knowledge she possessed.

For a moment, it seemed her heart would crack and break.

She packed up the clay chips in the barka leaf bag and lit a small fire to burn Be's ragged clothing. She left the cave and climbed down to the tree line, where Oats waited. She was not alone. Wonder had found them. She whinnied as Mave approached, and Mave's heart leaped at the horse's presence and from being recognized by two other beings.

"Oh, Wonder," she said, burying her face in her horse's neck.

Oats stamped the ground and swung her head toward the sky. The rain had stopped, and a thin band of clearing showed in the western sky. Again Oats stamped her foot, and Wonder pulled away from Mave's hold and began pawing the ground.

"All right," she said, "we'll go."

She felt at her neck that familiar cool feeling and the sensation that Tear's hand was there. She tried to brace herself for living in a world where sensations and memory would have to pass for human or lizard warmth.

Not with me along, you won't, Mave heard in her head.

She turned. There stood Tear.

"Tear," Mave said, laughing and crying at the same time, and threw her arms around her warm green shoulders. Tear melted into her and slid her arms around Mave's waist.

How? Mave sent the words to her. *I thought you'd gone below with the Ssha.*

I did. But you were tied to me, and that pulled me out. I got out just as they sealed the cave.

Mave touched the spikes of Tear's hair.

We'll travel under cover of night, Tear said, her mind to Mave's, *but even so, you'd better cover your head.*

Mave lay the battered purple cloth on her head, the remnant of Beatt's cape she'd earlier pounded into raggedness with a rock.

Tear stood close to Mave and straightened the square of rough fabric on her head. Tear smelled of lime, like the scrolls, but also of the warm earthiness of skin.

Tear left the front edge hanging over her eyes then joined Mave under the tent of cloth. She moved her head close to Mave's and grazed her lips in a kiss. Tear stepped back, smiled, and adjusted the fabric so the front hung just above Mave's eyes.

The four of them made their way down Ssha Mountain in the violet dusk. At the bottom, Mave swung onto Oats and smiled at Tear as she climbed on Wonder. Mave doubted she would ever return to Ssha Mountain, at least physically. But already she could feel the Ssha's vibrations, as though several hearts beat inside her chest. As her mother had instructed her to do, she let the vibrations become images, then words: courage, faith in the Ssha, and love. Then she let the vibrations shimmer through her, course through her veins like blood. She could feel everything in those pulsations, beginnings, endings, the magnificent and the mundane, everything and nothing. Turnip and others like him were out there somewhere, allies, perhaps. In the meantime, she had these two good beasts, Tear and herself, her body, heart, and mind all ready, she hoped, to go out into this newer, brighter world. The Great Mother's sun slipped below the horizon. One day it would rise again, like Venus in her morning return, but until then Mave had ten clay chips and a message to spread.

8
Gigante Love

THE HORSES, OATS AND WONDER, paused when they descended into the brush at the foot of Ssha Mountain. Tear looked at Mave. *Which way?* she asked Mave in mind-verse, cocking her head with its three-points of sculpted hair.

The filament of Tear's communication snaked into Mave's mind and branched off as a simple, surface question and a sizzle that ran from between her breasts to the bone arching over her bud. A third branch sought out the Ssha but Mave felt it hit the earth and break, like a flimsy arrow. Tear's aim was true but required a new ability she would need to succeed.

Mave let her essence melt into Oats' back and into the earth. *Which way?* she asked the Ssha.

Silence.

The plains lay ahead of them. To the east was Dia, burning. To the north was Apollonoulous. To the west lay the burial caves.

From Dia came a fresh wave of sooty smoke, blanketing Mave,

Tear, and the horses. Oats and Wonder snorted and shook their heads; Tear bent forward, coughing, over Wonder's neck.

Mave sneezed. She dabbed her tearing eyes then her nose with the hem of her head scarf. Her shoulders sagged in fatigue. She let her head drop to her chest, then brought it back up and turned to Tear.

Tear, who had recovered from her gulp of Gigante smoke, again asked Mave, in mind-verse, *Which way?*

A warm wind blew in from the west.

The caves, Mave said, nodding to the low mountains on their left, away from the coast and burning Dia. The caves were known to her and all in Dia, but only the women of hieros house entered them, which included those who had died and their spiritual sisters who buried them.

At the bottom of those low mountains, they swung off the horses. The four of them formed a line with Tear at the front and Wonder at the rear. Tear lead them up through the brambly olives trees that grew in a ring around the mountain. The sky had lightened from a deep blue to a dull turquoise when they reached the burial caves. They walked along the path until they reached the final cave. A meadow lay beyond it, and, above it, a grove of stout trees grew. A cascade of water fell from the tree grove through a well-worn V in the mountain between the cave and meadow, finally breaking on a ledge below. Tear hunted in the brush until she found a strip of bark, which she laid in the water stream to redirect it toward Oats and Wonder. Both horses had a long drink before wandering off to eat grass and the yellow-flowered weeds known to last well into the changing seasons. Tear and Mave took turns drinking and splashing themselves under the stream of water.

As the tips of the meadow grass turned red in the rising sun, Tear palmed Mave's eyes shut, then stood at her side and held her hand. As the sun inched upwards, Tear raised their clasped hands and together they took in the sun's energy.

Mave teetered, dizzy from the lack of sleep. Tear led her into the cave next to the meadow. Mave paused as they entered into the cool darkness that smelled of lime. Her stomach tightened with her old fear of darkness. Tear squeezed her hand then dipped her head close to Mave's and kissed her, a warm and quick press. Distracted, Mave let Tear lead her into the cave.

The temperature dropped every few steps they took. The cave was about forty paces deep and ended with a narrow berm of earth. Mave peered at the splotches of gypsum on its end and gasped.

"It's the mark of the hieros house women of Dia," she said, then repeated in mind-verse to Tear. Mave drew an outline in the air of the bouquet of long pods that grew like giant pea pods on the carob tree. *This is the burial place of women of hieros house*, she explained to Tear. *We're the first non-hieros house women to see this.*

Mave swayed as another wave of fatigue rolled over her. Tear motioned for her to sit and pulled two blankets and three capes from her pack, laying them out on the cave floor. She crawled under the top blanket and waited for Mave to join her. Mave crawled under the blanket and lay next to Tear, skin brushing against skin. Tear did not move. She wouldn't until Mave initiated a move. All half-and-halfs and all humans aged eighteen moons were initiated into the mysteries of the Ssha via sex with the local hieros house women. All humans but Mave. She'd gotten it directly from the source, a direct feed from the Ssha soul to hers. Unfortunately, that meant Mave knew very little about sex. Mave's body was ready but not her mind.

The women of hieros house had furnished their burial cave with two low stools for the mourners who sat in attendance for two moon rises after their sister's passing. A simple, two-tier shelf held what every grieving woman needs when away from home: a few cloths in case of out-of-cycle bleeding.

The next day Mave gratefully reached for one of the cloths left by the hieros house women when the familiar yet unexpected cramp signaled that her bleeding had begun. She was out of sync; her body usually stayed close to the full moon's rhythm, and this was the new moon.

Tear thrashed through the underbrush outside the cave, on a hunt for the latrine that Mave was sure the hieros house women had dug for their occasional visits. Mave slipped off her trousers and shirt and assembled a triangle of three cloths. She tied them together to form a circle then attached the ends of the third to the front and back of the circle. She stepped into it and readjusted the ties so that it snugged against her body. It would catch the seeping blood yet remain hitched just above her hip bones, where her waist curved in. She slipped on her trousers and top and sat on one of the stools.

Found it, Tear mind-versed as she strode into the cave, her face flushed. *Just below where the stream of water breaks. They tended the latrine after their last visit here; it's got a good layer of dirt on top. And when we need to tend it, we can use this.* She brandished a small shovel and smiled. *I found it laying near the latrine, along with this.* She held up a stick with a pointed piece of metal attached. *It'll be useful for digging hard dirt.*

Mave nodded, impressed. Tear was adapting quickly to the outer world.

I'll forage for food in the olive groves below and among the trees on the mountain top while you—Tear paused. She eyed Mave. *Have a rest on the stool?*

I'm bleeding, Mave explained.

Oh! Then you'll need leaves. I'll gather them while I'll find our breakfast. She charged out of the cave before Mave could tell her about her find.

When she returned with a pile of leaves Mave didn't have the heart to tell her she didn't need them quite yet. Mave kissed Tear softly on the lips and took the leaves from her. After Tear left, beaming, Mave slipped out of her cloth sling, not yet dotted with blood, though the tightening cramps told her it was making its way out of her body. Keeping on just her shirt, she sat on Tear's gift at the front of the cave which faced Dia. Gray, smoky mist hung over the town. Mave smelled the char of their burnings. Reluctantly, she breathed in the smoke. The tarry substance settled in her throat, causing it to momentarily seize up. She clutched at it, tried to call out for help but also in warning to Tear, but when her throat relaxed after a moment, she realized Tear was exposed to the smoke even more than she, being outside more. For a semi-divine half-and-half who had rarely left the Ssha caves in her nineteen years, Tear seemed born to the above-world. She spotted Tear as she moved between the olive trees. Somehow her muscles had become more pronounced overnight, and her shoulders had expanded and broadened.

Mother? Mave asked, sending her vibrational voice spidering out over the plain and into Dia. Faintly, she heard her mother's grunts and heaving breath. When her mother shouted, "Ha!" she knew her mother had triumphed over someone or something. But after the images and sounds, all went quiet.

Tear, Mave called to her in mind-verse.

When Tear's head popped out of the olive trees, Mave explained to her what she'd heard when she tried to connect with her mother, Audria, in mind-verse. Tear climbed up into the cave and put her hand over Mave's and listened with her.

After a few moments, Tear said in mind-verse, *I can't hear anything.* She smiled. *But then I don't bleed*, she said. *You can hear things I can't.*

Mave wasn't so sure about that. It was common for girls to travel more easily between worlds when bleeding, but Mave had had little practice navigating those realms. Tear looked expectantly at Mave, and Mave nodded, acknowledging Tear might be right. Tear brushed her lips across Mave's, then went back to foraging.

In the first moon cycle in their new home, Mave had a birthday. She was born at the time of year when the sun bowed to the moon, retreating into ever shorter days. Mave listened for but didn't hear anything from her mother. As the moon lost a slice of its light, Mave told Tear she was now a young woman. In the former Dia, she would have begun making choices, such as whether to take a mate or not. She would also be free to make manifest what the void rituals had taught her. However, because she had refused to attend these, she had only a very basic knowledge of what happened between bodies.

Tear continued to lay next to her at night, waiting for her to make a move. Mave did not feel ready and lay with her arms pinned to her sides.

The smoke from the Gigante's fires or siege continued to drift across the plain. Tear took in the sooty air, spending much of her time outside, foraging for food.

As the moon finished its dying, and Mave finished bleeding, Tear said to her in a croaky voice, "Should we go to Dia tomorrow?"

"Yes," she said, turning to Tear. "I think I'm ready." Then her jaw dropped in astonishment. "You spoke!"

Tear smiled. *That's the only sentence I can say aloud*, she said, in mind-verse. *I've been practicing.*

The sun, rain, and air had softened the piney green shade of Tear's skin to a dusky olive. The gills at her jaw line seemed less pronounced. The spikes of hair on her head had grown a bit and were starting to lay down rather than crest her head in the three points. Her chest and arms had grown strong from all the work she was doing to make their new home. The pearly scale on either side of her jaw lost its sheen and curled up around the edge.

That night, when Tear lay down beside Mave at the back of their cave, Mave took her hand and laid it on the soft skin of her thigh. That was as far as she felt ready to go.

Mave woke the next morning and rolled over to lay close to Tear, who lay still, waiting. Mave's body responded but she didn't want to get distracted from their purpose, traveling into Dia. Tear kept her eyes shut. Mave lay her cheek against Tear's and stared at the wall she lay next to. The first rays of the sun shone in the cave, illuminating the wall where bits of gold twinkled.

"Tear," Mave said, in spoken words, "look. There's something gold and sparkling where the wall meets the floor."

Tear opened her eyes and turned her head. She ran her hand along the base of the wall and brought back a handful of gravel. She and Mave rose and stood at the opening to the cave. Tear held out what she'd gathered: several small rocks colored with frosty white, black, and gold.

"Gold quartz," Mave said.

The women of Apollonoulous use it to trade for goods on the northern coast, Tear responded in mind-verse.

"We could sell or trade it, like the women of Apollonoulous do," said Mave. "Let's gather up as much as we can and take it along when we go into Dia. Who knows when we might need it, and it's better to be prepared."

Mave knelt near the seam in the wall where the gold quartz lay and dug her hands into the rough rocks, sweeping them into piles. The rising sun shone into the cave. Tear jumped up and hauled Mave to standing by the waist and lurched with her to the front of the cave. There she swung their clasped hands up to take in first light.

Mave pulled her hand out of Tear's grasp. "I want to dig for the gold quartz," she said aloud.

Tear snatched Mave's hand back and thrust their joined hands skyward. Mave was too stunned to say or do anything but stand before the sun in Tear's grip, like a rabbit in a hungry hawk's talons.

When Tear lowered their arms, Mave remained frozen, still in bunny mode, prey recently released. Tear turned away from Mave and started down the short cliff to the brushy area below their cave to forage for food. Mave's stomach growled. She followed. Tear would not look at her as they gathered the deep purple and ruby red berries, for fresh eating this morning and for drying into currants to eat throughout the winter and spring. Mave gathered the sage-green rugula leaves, and Tear dug small, sweet onions.

Soon the olives will be ripe enough to eat off the trees, Mave said in mind-verse to Tear.

Silence.

Mave faced Tear's stiff back as they trudged to their cave. Tear sat at the cave entrance and kept her head down while she ate. Mave was very confused. She didn't know how to interpret this new behavior.

I don't know what I did, but I'm sorry, Mave said in mind-verse to Tear, placing her hand atop Tear's.

Without looking up, Tear nodded.

Can you tell me what I did? Why you're upset?

You wanted to gather the gold quartz, I wanted to light. I wanted you to want what I wanted.

Mave considered this. It made no sense to her, but she tried to understand it for Tear's sake. After pondering for a few moments, she felt no more enlightened.

I don't understand how that would work, was all Mave could mind-verse to Tear.

Again Tear nodded, her forehead dropping sorrowfully down.

Mave couldn't bear the waves of sadness emanating off Tear. *I'll try*, Mave said. *I'll try to want what you want.*

Tear raised her head and a beaming smile spread across her face. She swooped in for a peck on Mave's cheek. *Let's go.*

Mave said her goodbye to Oats and Wonder as Tear packed their bags. Oats and Wonder were still in their stable, an arrangement of dead trees and branches Tear had put together as a small shelter for them. Mave and Tear had covered the ground in soft moss. Mave pulled up two handfuls of grass at the edge of the meadow then stood between Oats and Wonder and let them munch the green grasses in her hands. The yellow-flowered weeds Oats and Wonder liked so well grew more sparsely now, eclipsed by the spiny orange and pink daisies which they couldn't eat without cutting their mouths. Both horses looked thin, each of their ribs defined under their hides. The stream of water Tear had diverted to the meadow ran in a weaker runnel, but the seep below collected the water for the horses to drink. Mave didn't want them near the Gigante. The Gigante wrapped their horses in tight leather straps and struck them with whips.

"Let's go to Dia," Tear said behind Mave in a voice growing ever deeper.

Mave turned, smiling at the sound of her flinty voice. *Let's go*, she said in mind-verse.

"Yes, let's go," Tear said aloud. *You'll need this*, she said in mind-verse, dangling a battered, grayish-purple cloth, the remnant from Beatt's cape.

She pulled Mave toward her and placed the cloth on her head, winding a ragged strip just above her eyebrows to secure it. Tear turned away from Mave and headed down the mountain. Mave kept her eyes on Tear's feet through the narrow channel of sight the scarf afforded and followed her down the path through the olive trees to the plain below.

The morning breezes kept them cool as they crossed the plain. Mave lifted the back of her head scarf to cool her neck which ached from its perpetual bow.

As they neared Dia, the smell of fires grew stronger. Little ashy particles floated in the air they breathed.

We'll come in from the eastern docks, Tear said in mind-verse.

Why? Mave asked.

Tear's easy stride changed to a stomp as she shifted direction. Mave heard nothing back in reply.

They skirted Dia and approached the upper docks, signaled by the briny smell of the sea and, at the cliff's edge, the hooks that held a rope ladder. The sand and docks lay below. Though not ideal, it was the only place along the eastern coast to dock a boat.

Tear grabbed Mave and crashed with her on a stack of what looked like hunks of dirt with bits of dried grass.

Tear! Mave shouted to her in mind-verse, pushing her away so she could breathe. *What are you doing?*

Mave heard the rhythmic walking of several pairs of feet approached them, singing:

What do you do with a drunken sailor?
What do you do with a drunken sailor?
What do you do with a drunken sailor?
Ear-ly in the morning.

The tune was catchy, each line thrumming with the same percussive beat. It was music a person could work to. Only the women of hieros house had sung in Dia and not in a catchy way. Each woman sang a long, drawn-out "Oh" in tones different from the other, creating not harmony but strange and beautiful sounds. They sang together but in such a way to hide the singing's true purpose.

Tear squashed Mave against the stack of dried dirt and grass. The marching, singing men seemed almost to fall on top of them, then at the last moment they veered off, heading toward the cliff. Their voices descended as they climbed down the rope ladder to the dock.

Tear pulled Mave up, then, after making certain no dock workers were nearby, pulled her head scarf back over her face, obscuring her sight once again.

Anger and irritation bubbled up. *Is this what the Ssha initiation is for?* she thought to herself. *To get me accustomed to wearing a head scarf and never again see the path in front of me?*

Mem, she heard. *Mem*.

Anta! Mave shouted in her mind. Anta was alive, and she'd found Mave.

Tear strode ahead, pulling Mave by the arm.

Tear, Mave said in mind-verse. "Tear," she said aloud.

Tear spun around. "Not safe," she spat.

Yanking Mave's arm and holding her close, Tear maneuvered them into the thin stream of people heading toward Dia's new marketplace. The columns of black smoke were concentrated at the other end of the town.

Anta, Mave cried out in mind-verse. *I'm here. Where are you?*

The stream of people thickened. They had to be Mave's people; she could see flashes of the backs of their brown legs, though some men's legs were covered in dun-colored trousers, like the Gigante. How could people have adjusted so quickly?

We trained them too well, came Anta's voice. Her voice was like a bird's as it sang through damaged vocal cords. Her voice, once something sweet and pliable like warm sap, now was as hard and brittle as resin.

Anta! Here I am. Where are you? Mave clung to Tear's arm as the thickening crowd jostled and pressed against her.

A woman's bare, brown arm appeared in Mave's tunnel of sight and reached for Tear's arm. Tear ground to a halt. The woman led Tear to the round, stone pod that had once been Dia's hieros house, home to Anta and her sisters in spirit. Anta pushed Tear and Mave into a small space near the entrance, and they hunkered down to hide from passers-by.

Cautiously, Mave lifted the edge of her head scarf and peered out. A woman seated herself on the stone step, her back ramrod straight, and arranged her red skirt around her brown calves. Mave's throat constricted, as though she experienced the ruin of damaged vocal cords. It was Anta.

"Mem," Anta whispered. "I can't turn around. If a Gigante comes, I must bring him inside. They like their sex with theater, so we go along with the drama. They need a houseful of women ready to obey and serve them. We don't have to wear head scarves because we don't belong to one man but all men."

"Then nothing's changed," Mave said in a whisper, as she crouched next to Tear.

"The rules have changed," Anta whispered. "It's true, here in Dia as before the Gigante, the women of hieros house are free to join with any man. But if a woman isn't of hieros house, she must belong only to one man. If she doesn't, she automatically belongs to all men. Either way, the Gigante require their submission." She laughed softly. "It's similar to how they view their horses." She paused. "They renamed us. They call us House of Hor, after a goddess in lands farther east of us."

The bulging calves of a Gigante came into view. He towered over Anta. Her skirt rustled as she stood.

Anta, where is my mother? Mave asked in frantic mind-verse.

Mave raised her head a few cautious inches. *Anta*, she tried to shout with her mind.

Anta ran her palm along the Gigante's arm, then slid her hand up and down his outer thigh. All standard stuff for a woman of hieros house beginning an initiation into Ssha mysteries. That purpose had gone undercover, and so had the women of hieros house.

The Gigante clamped his big hand around Anta's neck. The tips of his big fingers almost touched as he gripped her throat and pushed her ahead of him into the House of Hor. Silence.

Mave couldn't take in what she'd just witnessed, like a small animal just learning the ways of the kingdom of beasts. Her heart rended, causing a physical pain. She bowed her head and pressed her hand to her chest.

Tear rose up slowly next to Mave, then led her away from Anta and the former hieros house. *Let's go home*, Tear said.

They left Dia without any sign of Mave's mother. They ate their fruit as they walked across the plain, with the sun bearing down on them. Mave's scalp simmered under her head scarf. She was happy to eat fruit, and the ache in her chest faded though the memory of heart break remained.

A rumbling cart passed them, heading toward their low mountain. Mave raised her head slightly to see the cart as it passed them. Two horses pulled the cart, driven by a Gigante with a whip. The cart held about ten people of Dia, people Mave thought she recognized but couldn't be sure. It was a mix of women and men. The men kept their heads bowed like the women in their head scarves.

By the time Mave and Tear reached the bottom of their low mountain, the Gigante cart had already arrived and unloaded its workers. The ten people of Dia had climbed up into the olive groves, where the fall fruit was ripe and ready to pick.

The Gigante man huddled at the bottom near the cart. He roused at Mave and Tear's approach.

"Up," he shouted, jabbing a finger at the olive pickers.

He thinks we're workers, Tear said to Mave in mind-verse.

They kept their heads bowed and joined their former townspeople spread out among the twisted arms of the olive trees. Mave stood next to a woman and both picked the fruit silently.

"Mavealeph?" the woman asked softly.

"Yes," Mave whispered back in surprise.

She nodded. "We've been waiting for you."

Mave was astonished but kept her arms moving rhythmically, picking the olives for the Gigante. Tear made her way farther up through the groves to join the men at the top row of trees.

"I'm Nemmis. The women of hieros house—House of Hor—told us to look for you. They said you would know what to do next."

Nervously, Mave looked down at the Gigante fellow. He hunched over his crossed arms.

Nemmis took Mave's hand. "He won't come up here. The Gigante are afraid of the caves above the olive groves."

"Why?" Mave asked.

She giggled. "We told them they're haunted by the dead we bury there. They fear the bones of the dead rising up. That's why they burn their dead."

"Is that why there's always a fire burning in Dia?"

"Partly." She paused. "To keep their god happy, they burn small animals."

Mave felt sick. She and Tear had been breathing in the Gigante dead and their burnt sacrifices.

"They brought two priests, Lewi and Levi, who direct the sacrifices," Nemmis continued. "I've heard their god sits on a mountain top and hurls thunderbolts."

Mave gathered everything Nemmis told her in a message to the Ssha, imagining the words traveling along a vibrating string down through her sternum and out the bottoms of her feet into the ground. She waited. Silence. No Ssha vibration tunneled back to her. She felt for her mother, groping about with her mind. More silence.

"Next new moon," Mave whispered to Nemmis. "We'll gather in the tree grove above the caves." Mave had no idea if this was the move to make or not, but clearly it was up to her to begin plans. "Will you and the others be able to get away?"

The young woman tied off her full bag of olives and pulled an empty bag from her belt. "We'll tell the Gigante the new moon is the best time for picking olives. We'll send two at a time up to you. We can take turns keeping watch. The Gigante shout rather than talk, so you'll hear them if they rouse or tell us picking is done." She turned to look down at the Gigante guard below. "I'll make a commotion now so you and your mate can get back to your cave."

Mave climbed to the top row of olive trees that grazed the stone path to the caves. Tear crouched behind the spiny arms of a bush. They met each other's eyes. Tear, as Mave had first known her, looked back at her. Mave smiled.

Nemmis shouted and crashed down through the trees. The startled Gigante guard leaped off the cart and, body rigid, watched her make her way down.

"Spirits!" Nemmis shouted. "I heard them."

The Gigante's white face went whiter. "Enough picking for today," he shouted. "Everyone in the cart."

While the others made their way down to the cart, Tear and Mave quickly edged around the path and into their cave. They lay side by side at the front and watched the Gigante drive the cart full of workers across the plain in the final rays of the day's sun. Without raising her covered head, Nemmis waved quickly then tucked her hand back in her lap. She whirled in her seat to face the Gigante driver.

"The spirits," she shouted, "they're chasing us!"

Tear and Mave laughed as the Gigante driver jumped several inches off his seat. Their smiles faded and Mave's stomach twisted as the Gigante driver snapped a whip against the horse's flank to send him streaming toward Dia.

Mave and Tear checked on Oats and Wonder, who munched grass close to their stall. Mave and Tear stood together under the sluicing water, washing themselves as well as their clothing. They sat on soft moss at the front of the cave and ate ripe olives, rugula, and onions. The sun had fully set and the dying moon rose heavily in the sky. Soon she would fade to a sliver then nothingness, and then, when the moon was new and prey was safe, Mave and the others would gather.

Tear covered Mave's hand with hers. *There's work in Dia*, she said in mind-verse. *The pickers told me the Gigante always need new men—or a person they think is a man, like the pickers thought I was—on the cart crew. They haul a lot from their boats below Dia and the work is hard, so many men don't last long. I'm stronger now than when I lived inside Ssha Mountain.*

And taller, Mave added.

I can learn a lot working on the crew, Tear continued as though she hadn't heard Mave.

Mave gazed off at the greasy smoke staining the dark blue sky black. The evening breezes blew the smoke their way. Her lungs filled with the Gigante dead.

Tear clamped her hand down on Mave's neck, like the Gigante had done to Anta. Mave pulled away, angry. Tear looked startled and let her hand drop.

They soon lay down on their soft bedding at the back of the cave.

Gigante love, Tear said in mind-verse.

"Not for us," Mave said aloud. *Not for us,* she said again in mind-verse.

"Nee for oos," Tear said aloud, in the language of the Gigante.

She and Mave lay with a large gap of empty space between them.

When Mave woke, the cave was dark but tinged with the dawn's light. She turned her head, and Tear lay there, looking at her. Something bubbled up in her. She turned on her side and reached down to stroke Tear's bud, but Tear moved her hand away. Tear clambered to her hands and knees and climbed on top of Mave. Tear's warmth felt good, soothing, but the full weight of her body felt strange and foreign to Mave. She couldn't tell if she liked it or not. She parted her legs and let Tear lie between them.

Tear's male part, her stem, grew hard. She pressed it against Mave's bud, creating a pleasurable tingling. Mave tilted her pelvis up and Tear pushed inside. Tear thrust rhythmically in and out, and Mave rocked with her. The tingling in Mave's bud grew to lightning strikes. Tear buried her face in Mave's neck and quickly reached her peak. She fell against Mave, then rolled off and lay next to her.

Tear said aloud in her flinty voice that was quickly losing its croak, "Gigante love for oos."

Tear fell asleep, snoring loudly. Mave stared up at the cave's ceiling for a time, wondering what she was supposed to feel. The act with Tear felt good, but it now seemed momentary, as though a rarely used channel had opened and then closed. Now that it had closed, she quickly returned to her usual self.

She patted the floor beside her, searching for a rag to put

under her, for the blood that would surely come. Finding none within her reach, she rolled over to look on Tear's side. Propped up on her elbow, peering into the soft light, her eye was caught by the absence of iridescence along Tear's jaw. The pearly scales on either side of Tear's jaw had fallen off and disappeared into the tangle of blankets.

9
Bag of Ruin

THE NEXT MORNING IN THE pre-dawn darkness, Mave groped for the clay chips, little ciphers of her making. Her hand found the bag Beatt had given her and she drew it close. She loosened the drawstring top as she lay next to Tear and carefully shook the ten clay chips on her chest. Tear slept deeply, her snores like a deer in rut. The Ssha's knowledge was secure on her clay chips, but if she couldn't transmit it, what was the point? *Mother*, thought Mave, *where is your bad advice when I need it?* Mave put the chips bag in their bag, then burrowed into Tear's warm side and called on the invisible legions—spirits trapped in trees, presences hovering.

The wind lowed like a mourner. Mave lay still against Tear. She waited for tears to come, to relieve the watery pressure behind her eyes. Nothing.

Sister Aleph, came a raspy voice in Mave's mind.

Sister Ssha! Mave shot up to sitting and hurled her voice in response as though it were a thunderbolt. She aimed the strike out over the plain toward Ssha Mountain and deep into the dirt.

Mave pressed her palm on Tear's forearm. Tear's eyes opened. She grinned slyly and slipped her hand beneath Mave's tunic, her palm calloused from shoveling fresh dirt on the latrine and picking olives.

"Not now," Mave said, lifting Tear's hand away. "It's Sister Ssha, I can hear her calling me."

Tear rolled Mave onto her back.

Mave pushed her off and struggled to sitting. "Tear! It's the Ssha!"

Tear rose. She stretched. Her body was long and lean, and her olive skin had a sheen in the early-morning light. Her hair, which grew quickly above-ground, grazed her shoulders.

"I'll wait for you at the front," she said and pulled on her tunic and trousers.

Mave closed her eyes. *Sister Ssha?* she asked. *I'm here.*

Silence.

Mave rose from their pile of blankets and stood behind Tear at the cave entrance. A gray haze hung over Dia. Staring at it instead of the rising sun, Tear raised up her arms and took in the energy the Gigante fires offered. Mave turned away from Tear and toward the sun inching above the horizon, raising her arms to its warmth.

Without a word, Tear charged out of the cave. *Not again*, thought Mave, What else could Tear's abrupt and sullen departure be but anger at Mave not wanting what Tear wanted? Mave followed her down the path. She was of two minds, one that was tired of Tear's sudden mood shifts and one that just wanted the return of peace. They silently foraged for rugula and onions. Mave watched Tear for a sign of what she had done wrong. Instead of a glower and stern set of her lips, Tear's expression seemed neutral, impassive, as she held open her hands to Mave to display her bounty of onions. Happy that Tear didn't seem upset, Mave leaned in to kiss her. When Tear did not return the gentle press, Mave pulled away. Tear's face was tight, as though she were restraining herself. *Let's eat*, she mind-versed to Mave and turned back toward their cave where they ate in an uneasy silence.

Tear and Mave ate then bathed in the collected rainwater near Oats and Wonder's makeshift stable. They kept their tunics and trousers on and washed those along with themselves.

While Tear rinsed her trousers under the stream of water, Mave walked out to where Oats and Wonder stood in the meadow. She ran her hands along their sides as they sandwiched her between them.

Tear wrung the water out of her trousers and top and sang, practicing her words:

What do you do with a drunken sailor

What doo yoo doo with a drunken sailor

Oooowwwhat do ya do with a drunken sailor…

Mave patted the horses' necks and climbed up to the grove. The wind lifted the boughs of the evergreen trees, and the needles gently scratched Mave's leg. Tonight, when the moon was new, Mave would host a secret gathering among these trees and use her will to drive the Ssha energy to rise up like sap.

They woke after sunset. The sky shaded to dark blue then the near black of a moonless night. Tear and Mave sat at the front of the cave. They listened for the wheels of the Gigante work cart. Tear lay her hand on Mave's thigh.

The wind from the east kicked up, carrying the smell and soot of the Gigante fires across the plain and up into their cave. A cry of "Whoa" sounded in the distance. The Gigante wagon lumbered toward them. The Gigante's leather saddle squeaked while the wagon planks groaned as it was pulled up to the mountain.

The Gigante driver shouted, "Down! Get to work." As the workers got off the cart and climbed up into the olive grove, the Gigante built a fire and sat by it. Shortly, he lay down next to it, and Mave watched his body relax in the warm firelight as he fell asleep.

Tear crawled down the stone path then dropped into the olive groves. Mave waited on the edge of the path. Soon Nemmis, the young woman Mave had met picking olives, crawled up to meet her. Only when she faced Mave did she pull back her head scarf, and then only to whisper an excited, "Hello!" before pulling it back down. Another young woman joined them, and whispered hello from underneath her head scarf.

The three of them climbed up the mountain on the side between Tear and Mave's cave and the horses' pasture. When they reached the top, they stood at the edge of the grove. None of them had ever climbed up to the grove before. From Dia they could always see it, still and green at all times of year. They believed the spirits of their buried ancestors kept it green, the color of the Ssha's scaly bodies.

The wind shifted again, blowing the smell of the fires back to Dia.

"Thank you, Ssha," Mave whispered, and Nemmis and the other young woman echoed her.

They walked into the grove a little way until they found a small clearing. The trees curved over them in a canopy. The wind swept the trees' low-hanging boughs back and forth like brooms. The three stood together in a small circle. Nemmis and the young woman were draped in cloth, no skin showing except their hands; they could have passed for statues.

We're here, Mave moisoved to the Ssha. *Sister Ssha, we're here.*

The wind whistled through the trees.

After a time of nothing happening, Nemmis said softly, "I'll go down and send another up."

"Me too," said the other, faceless young woman and quickly followed Nemmis out of the grove.

For the next few hours as the moon lay in darkness, keeping Mave and the Goddess safe to roam, two by two the workers came up and joined Mave in the grove. Just like with Nemmis and her young friend, they stood and waited while Mave stood and waited while nothing happened. Finally, after the last two departed, Tear joined her in the forest.

"They're gone," Tear said, putting her hand on Mave's shoulder.

Mave turned her head and pressed her cheek against Tear's warm hand. "So are the Ssha and the Goddess, I think."

Tear took Mave's hand and led her out of the grove and down the path to the meadow. When they reached the meadow, Tear turned. She lay Mave down in the grass and Mave let her grind her into the earth. She experienced the same slow pulse in her bud that grew to an explosion of feeling, stronger this time because of how hard Tear could pound with Mave's back against the giving earth. Afterwards, Tear rinsed her tunic and trousers under the runnel of water and brought Mave a blanket to pull around her while her clothing dried. They slept in the meadow that night with Oats and Wonder nearby.

The next new moon, Tear and Mave dutifully watched and listened for the Gigante cart lumbering across the plain to their mountain. None of the workers came up to the grove. Mave was too disheartened to climb down and speak with Nemmis. Tear did, though. She learned the Gigante were eager to lay in as many olives as they could before harvest ended. They had developed a taste for olive oil, Nemmis told Tear, not to eat but to sell. They had restricted how much Dia's citizens could consume.

They hired young boys to press the fruit in a contraption that pressed olives between bricks, paying only when the workers had extracted a certain amount into the flat pans beneath the presser.

When again the moon grew dark, the Gigante cart trundled up to their mountain. Mave sat in the cave while Tear climbed down to speak with Nemmis. Mave waited. She waited so long she drowsed then fell asleep. The shouts of the Gigante driver woke her. As he stamped out his fire, he called for the workers to climb back aboard. Tear climbed up through the spiky olive trees.

"They promise more money to those who pick the most," Tear said as they watched the cart rumble over the plain back to Dia.

Mave laughed. "Then the Gigante win," she said. "I don't have any money to offer. I can't give anyone a job." She tossed the barka bag of chips over her shoulder. It landed behind them in the cave. "I have no idea what I'm doing."

"Do you use the chips?" Tear asked.

"During the ritual?" Mave asked.

Tear nodded.

"No," Mave said, "I haven't. Do you think I should?"

Tear nodded. "Turnip said you should."

She turned to her in surprise. "Was Turnip here tonight?"

Tear shook her head. "He sent a message through Nemmis."

"So everyone knows what a bad job I'm doing?"

Tear shook her head. "I think Turnip is trying to help."

"How do we get anyone to attend the rituals?" Mave asked. "The olive pickers had a few feet to climb, and they decided it wasn't worth the effort."

"We'll ask Turnip." Tear stood and pulled Mave up with her. *Tomorrow, we'll go to Dia*, she said in mind-verse. *You talk to Turnip, and I'll get a job.*

Mave started bleeding the next day, sooner than expected. Her body was still out of sync with the moon. Tear gathered leaves and brought them to her inside the cave. Tear sat with Mave, knee to knee, and held her hands, palms up, in her hands.

"Close your eyes," Tear said. "Women are more sensitive to Ssha vibrations when they're bleeding."

"How would you know?" Mave asked. "Whatever was female in you has gone away."

Tear grinned.

"My stomach hurts," Mave said, and took herself and a fresh pile of leaves into the horses' sparse stable. Tear did not follow her. Oats and Wonder saw her and ambled over to join her. Held steady by her horses' warm bodies, she let her muscles sag, and at that moment the Lizard People's vibrations flooded in, a hard rain pummeling the soles of her feet. The spindles traveled up her legs, into her torso and arms and along the sides of her neck then blasting out of her head. Both Oats and Wonder shook their heads as though bees buzzed in their manes.

Please speak to me, Mave pleaded to the Ssha in mind-verse. *No one's coming to the rituals, and I don't know how to keep the Ssha message alive. The Gigante offer jobs*, she ranted, *and everyone wants those.*

No words came in return. Just vibrations. Mave sat still as they rocked her body. After a time, they drained out of her.

Wonder settled into sleep, and Oats took the first watch. Mave lay there a little while longer feeling the warmth of her horses' bodies and holding the memory of the vibrations.

She joined Tear in the cave, at the back where she waited on their bed of blankets and old capes. Mave spread one of the cloths left by the women of hieros house on her side, then lay down naked beside Tear. Mave could not find Tear's female part, that pearl of flesh in the folds of skin between her legs. She could only find her stem. In Mave's hand, her stem grew, bigger, it seemed, than the last time Mave had stroked it to hardness.

Afterwards, as Tear slept, Mave looked at the faint glow of the gold quartz lining the back corner of the cave. The gold quartz could bring them money, and if they had money, they didn't need Gigante jobs.

The next morning, the wind whispered through the boughs of the trees as they lighted. The sun cast its late-season rays on the gray, wintry waters off the eastern coast, reflecting a dull glaze back on the sky. The trees in the grove above pulled Mave toward them.

"Let's wait to go into Dia," Mave said. "Can you get a message to Turnip through Nemmis?"

Tear said nothing, aloud or in mind-verse, and just nodded and stared out across the plain at Dia and the ever-present smoky cloud hovering above it. She climbed down a few ledges and began throwing fresh dirt on their latrine.

Mave climbed up to the trees. The rhythm of changing seasons was strong in the grove. If Mave looked at the trees out of the corner of her eye, she seemed to catch them in different forms, as though they weren't really trees but spirits frozen in tree form.

Each day Mave went back to their cave as the sun set, where Tear waited with food. Mave seemed to have run out of words. She only wanted to be back in the grove. Tear became subdued, quiet, also without words, spoken or thought, and fell in with Mave's rhythm. At night, though, her body seemed to spring to attention the moment they lay down on their bed of capes. For several moon cycles in the morning they lighted then Mave returned to the forest above. Tear got word to Turnip through Nemmis that their trip into Dia was delayed.

One evening when Mave returned to the cave Tear wasn't there. Mave walked along the path calling Tear's name. When the sun set, she went back to the cave. She ate the fresh olives, rugula, and onion that Tear had put inside for her.

When she woke the next morning, Tear was back. They lighted together, and Mave felt the excitement in Tear's hand as they raised up their arms.

Mave followed Tear down the path to forage. Tear strode down, her hair long enough to swing back and forth as she walked. They both knelt in the dirt and dug for onions.

Tear shook the dirt off two onions and handed one to Mave. "I got a job," Tear said aloud. "Nemmis helped me sneak on the Gigante cart yesterday. I went into Dia with them. I'm going to work on the Gigante cart crew." She went on in mind-verse: *I'll unload their boats docked below the cliff on the eastern edge.* She smiled at Mave then restlessly dug for more onions.

Worry niggled in the pit of her gut. She didn't see how any good could come of Tear being around the Gigante. But Tear would be paid in the Gigante coin, and Mave knew they would need those coins one day and probably sooner than later. She used this thinking to push away the thought that she was happy to get time alone, to get a taste of the solitude she had once taken for granted.

For several moon cycles, Tear rode the cart into Dia at the start of her work week. The olive harvest for the season was done, but the Gigante brought workers to Mave and Tear's low mountain for another project: digging long rows in the dirt. The rain collected into the new rows the workers dug. Mave spent her days among the trapped spirits of trees. She spoke only to murmur to Oats and Wonder. She slept alone on their blankets at the back of their cave with only the still and silent spirits of the dead hieros women for company. Tear came back to their cave at the work week's end. Mave welcomed Tear's body when she returned, moving easily from her role as solitary female to lover. She no longer searched for Tear's bud and when Tear placed her hand on her growing stem learned how to stroke in such a way that Tear rocked and moaned. The movements that Tear liked best were the most mechanical, and Mave discovered she could perform these with her hands and those with her body when Tear thrust in her yet hold her heart and mind apart. With that protective guard in place, Mave found peace with this phase of her new life.

The winter winds warmed. When Tear appeared one morning, at her work week's end, she handed Mave a vial. Mave uncorked it and sniffed. "Castor and almond oil," she said, smiling broadly.

"The Gigante won't sell us olive oil but they don't mind if we make our own. Women sell it in the marketplace now."

Mave's smile faded. "You spent your wages on hair oil?"

Tear stiffened. "It's a gift for you. It was supposed to make you happy."

"Of course, of course, I'm sorry," Mave said and buried her face in her hands. She raised her head and placed her palms on Tear's cheeks. "It does. And now that I've got hair oil, I can go into Dia with you."

Tear nodded. She led Mave back to their bed.

The next day they rose early, while the sky was still dark. Tear pulled on her trousers and top, and Mave oiled her fingers and ran them through her hair. When the curls lay shining along her neck and grazing her shoulders, she lay a large square of cloth on her head with the edge hanging low, just above her eyebrows. She tied a ragged ribbon of fraying hemp around her head to secure the cloth. When Tear was ready, they paused at the entrance to their cave.

"Should we light?" Mave asked.

Tear looked off into the smoky distance. "We don't go underground anymore; that's what it was for. It probably doesn't matter whether we light or not."

Mave couldn't argue with that, but the loss of yet another old way of life hung heavy on her heart. Would life just hurt from now on?

Tear helped Mave shoulder her bag with fruit and a clay cup to dip into the wells in Dia.

Before they set off, Tear said, "We'll need a signal for danger." To Mave's puzzled look she said, "Things can shift suddenly in Dia. I don't know if it's the same in Apollonoulous, but you have to be ready for trouble in Dia. If I see something amiss, I'll pull on your arm, like this." She yanked on Mave's arm.

"Ow!" Mave said, pulling her arm out of Tear's grasp and rubbing it. "That hurt!"

"Sorry," Tear said as she shouldered her bag of fruit and her clay cup. "It's what the Gigante expect." She turned and headed off on the path.

They made their way down the mountain and into town. With each step, Mave let her head drop a little farther. By the time they reached the western edge of Dia, her chin grazed her chest, and her eyes watched only her feet.

She smelled the fires first. She raised her head to sneak a look. Two boys with singed eyebrows held clay bowls under the animal being sacrificed. Two men wearing identical black robes with sleeves so long they grazed their wrists stood watch over the boys. The two men wore stoles of crimson and violet, shiny strips of color hanging like yokes around their necks.

Head down, Tear said to Mave in mind-verse and pressed on the back of her skull. *The boys take the fat to the women who cook for the Gigante*, Tear continued. *The two men are Gigante priests, Lewi and Levi.*

As Tear lead her through the marketplace, Mave raised her head just enough to catch glimpses of faces beneath the head scarves. The head turned a certain way, the sun flashed on features of a face, and, she thought, I know you! The looks were too brief, however, to be sure. Heads dipped quickly back to the ground, and the head scarves obscured faces. Mave looked beyond the market, to the south, where Anta and her sisters were in House of Hor. None of the women in their signature red skirts and bare heads were about.

The rubble of Mave's home lay beyond House of Hor. Beyond that stood the Gigante compound, several buildings built of brick with an animal yard, stables, and garden beyond it.

Turnip neighed like a horse when he saw them. He reared up and pawed the air with his cupped hands. He wore sashes of crimson and violet like those the Gigante priests, Lewi and Levi, wore. He pranced around Tear and Mave. Mave glanced up between her lashes. Tear stuck out her hand, and Turnip grasped it as though starting a wrestling match.

Mave dropped her bag. Turnip knelt to pick it up, and as he did, Mave bent down, and their heads met.

"We don't have much time," Turnip whispered. "I'm out on an errand for the Executrix. The Gigante demoted her to assistant administrator and gave her a pig lot to run. She lives in the Gigante compound, as do I." He paused, looking around. "We can sit here," he said, gesturing to a low stack of dirt cakes, the kind Mave had seen before at the docks. "No one can connect with the Ssha," he said. "No one knows why. I've even tried what worked for me the very first time I connected, but it didn't work. We've been holding out hope for you."

"Sometimes I think I feel the Ssha vibrations but then the feeling drains away," Mave said. "You think it might help to use my clay chips during the new moon ritual?"

Turnip nodded. "I did something like that when I connected the first time with the Ssha many years ago, when we still punished men for that. I'd traded for a scale that was supposed to have dropped off a Ssha. It was as big as a blossom and had a sheen like a green and black pearl. I looked at it, held it and just thought about it. After a time, my sense of self seemed to recede. Then I was a thread in a giant weave, connected to everything. Could you try that? Just hold one of the chips in your hand at the start of a new moon ritual?"

"I guess I can," Mave said. She couldn't picture how it would affect the ritual but she could try it. It felt strange to have a thing between her and Ssha energy.

"Can you go to Apollonoulous?" Turnip asked. "To their market? It's different there. You might find more who are interested in attending the rituals. Apollonoulous was ready for change in a way that Dia wasn't."

"So their hieros house wasn't renamed?" Mave asked.

"De-named, you might say," Turnip said. "No one calls them the women of hieros house anymore. They are just businesswomen. A few of them have taken Gigante as husbands."

Tear grabbed Mave's arm and yanked it upward. Mave glared at her from under her head scarf.

"Danger," Mave turned back to Turnip and whispered.

Turnip straightened then dusted off Mave's bag with broad, smacking sweeps, all the while grinning idiotically. He bent at the waist in a bow, handing Mave her bag.

She bent forward to accept it.

"We are safe if we go along," Turnip said. "The groves above your cave are safe; the Gigante fear the bones of our dead."

Tear jerked again on Mave's arm, hard enough to make her wince.

"A Maryannu's coming," Tear bent to whisper to Turnip.

Turnip leaned toward Mave. "Maryannu are the warriors who came with the Gigante. They drive chariots pulled by fast horses. They're trained in the use of swords. They'll chase down any living thing for the sport of it. They're always ready to do battle. If there isn't a fight going on, they'll start one. The Gigante pay them well. When they're not engaged, they roam about, stir up dust and alarm, and drink and eat, like those," Turnip said, nodding toward the men gathered at the end of the market. "Keep out of their way."

Turnip cantered off, the ends of his crimson and violet sashes fluttering.

Mave tipped her head back just far enough to watch the Maryannu driver and his horse-drawn chariot crash toward the marketplace. The crowd parted to allow him and his chariot through. Mave stood as the solitary rider passed. For a moment she thought the warrior looked like her mother but told herself she must have imagined it. She wanted to see her mother so much she was starting to imagine her. The Maryannu thundered past Mave and raced his chariot toward the other end of the marketplace where his fellow warriors cheered and raised their mugs. The people in the marketplace huddled together, mumbling to each other. The hisses of their whispers rose like the buzzing of cicadas.

The Maryannu wheeled around and roared back, scattering the people. "No roun," the warrior shouted.

Lewi and Levi, the priests who were accompanying the two boys with their full pans back to the compound, both whirled around, their black skirts and the ends of their stoles flapping.

"No whispering," shouted one priest.

"No secrets," shouted the other. "No roun."

The Maryannu retreated to where his comrades gathered at the end of the market. They had tethered their horses and chariots to a long post. Cheers went up as the Maryannu started a game of dice.

Mave clutched her bag of clay chips. She pushed past Tear and through the crowds of people flooding back in and ran on the packed dirt to where the Maryannu played dice. Mave skidded to a halt near the chariots, still tethered to their horses. The blinkered horses stared off into the distance. The four Maryannu paused in their game; four helmeted heads swiveled to look at Mave. She raised her arm, holding the bag of chips aloft. She stretched her arm back, preparing to hurl the bag at the warriors. The Maryannu who had arrived moments ago sprang up. He was shorter than the other three, with skin that had turned quickly brown under the southern sun. He strode to Mave and locked his hand, small in comparison to the others', around her wrist.

"Better not have roun," he growled, shaking her arm.

His comrades laughed and returned to their game.

"I have roun," Mave whispered, "a bagful." She shook the bag, rattling the chips, and the Maryannu gripped her forearm to stop the noise. "Go ahead," she said, "kill me."

The Maryannu drew close, bringing his caged brown face within inches of hers. His eyes filled with tears through the bars of his metal face plate. For a moment someone Mave knew swam in those eyes. *Mother?* she asked in mind-verse. The Maryannu bent her back, looming over her, his tears falling on the arm he twisted. Mave folded onto the ground in pain, and he stood over her, laughing, one sandaled foot pinning her down.

"She's a joker," he called to the other Maryannu. "The joker's making a game for us. Aren't you?" he asked, turning to look at her held under his foot.

He dug his foot into her hip. "Well?"

"Yes," she whispered, "I'm making a game for you."

"We want a game now," said one of the warriors without looking up from the dice game.

"Whoever guesses how many chips in her bag wins," the Maryannu standing over Mave said.

"Wins what?" asked the Maryannu.

"A fight with me," he shouted.

The Maryannu erupted. They jumped up from their dice game, bellowing and punching the air with their fists.

The short, sun-kissed man standing over Mave said, "Two moons," then stomped back to his men and swung at the first man he encountered.

In the noise and dust Mave crawled away with her bag of chips, armed with an order from a Maryannu whose tears dried on her arm.

10
Undercover Goddess

MAVE SAT SHELTERED FROM THE heat in her stall, looking for signs and stranded between pleasure and pain by the sound of Tear's flinty voice rising into song behind the stall.

The sun glinted off the red jewels in the headband of the woman across from Mave. She sold little verticals of amber liquid. She raised one of the vials and turned it this way and that in the burning, flat rays of the rising sun. The honeyed gold sparkled. The pert purple cloth the woman wore at her crown beat like dark blood.

Mave's barley-colored scarf and shift Tear had brought her from Dia kept her cool but invisible. She shook her dun-colored cup in the woman's direction, and the clay chips inside clicked.

"Naphtha oil from Gigante peat," the woman sang out.

Several of those traveling upstream on the woman's side of the market halted to look. Behind them the river of people surged and formed a logjam in front of the woman's stall, and their clamoring and waving arms swallowed up her and her glints of light.

"Games for sale," Mave mumbled at the current of people streaming down her side of the market. She shook her cup again, and the chips rattled like bones.

A boy popped out of the crowd, a little girl in tow. He dragged her with him to Mave's stall. Mave rose from her stool. The girl wore her head scarf pushed back on her head, a crown of cloth like the woman's, but a rich green.

"Dice?" the boy asked, squinting into the sun. "Like the Gigante play?"

Mave shook her head. "My game is better," she said. "My game chips have designs that hold secrets."

The boy's face settled into a frown. "We're not supposed to have roun," he said.

Mave stared at the boy, trying to determine if he were auguring good or ill.

"Secrets," the girl said helpfully to Mave.

"Come on," said the boy to his sister, taking her hand, "let's go before we get in trouble." The boy led the girl into the stream of people, and they disappeared.

"What do you do with a drunken sailor," Tear sang, and her fellow workers loading the Gigante cart parked behind the stall joined in.

After almost thirteen moon cycles living among the Gigante, Tear's voice had dropped several notes. It was now deep and ragged, like the cut rock on the eastern coast. Her time as a speechless, compliant, green-skinned, semi-divine half-and-half had ended.

The girl reappeared at Mave's stall holding the hand of her mother. The girl pointed to the cup with Mave's clay chips.

"My little girl would like to see your game," the mother said from under the folds of her head scarf hooded over her face.

Mave emptied the clay chips onto the narrow display table. One by one, she turned them face-up so their symbols were displayed. She turned them so both the girl and her mother could see them.

The mother let out a soft gasp.

The girl reached up and clicked two of the chips together. "I want this, mommy," she said.

"Ssh," her mother said, then raised her head so her eyes met Mave's. "Ssha?" she asked.

"Yes," Mave said in a jovial voice, a cheerful shopkeeper, "exactly right. I'm sure you know quality when you see it."

The mother reached out her hand as though to get a better look and swept several of the chips to the ground in the front of the stall. "I'm so sorry," she said, and dropped to her knees to pick them up while the girl watched.

Mave's chips were as solid as stone and they would not break. Mave knew; she had tried several times to crush them. Abuse seemed to sustain rather than break them.

Mave came around to the front of the table and knelt next to the mother. Mave bowed her head next to hers. "Old moon?" she asked, the first line of coded exchange.

"Never old moon," said the mother. "Only always new."

Mave handed the girl one of the clay chips, a new one she'd created in addition to the original ten she'd made in the Ssha caves. This new chip showed a cat-like creature with horns asleep on a human's chest. "A charm," Mave said to the girl, "for good luck."

The girl happily grabbed the chip and held it tight in her hand. After a moment, she unfurled her fingers to gaze at the image on the chip.

"My name is Inna," the mother said.

"I'm Mavealeph," Mave said.

"I know," Inna said, "daughter of Dia's star counsel." She turned her head sideways, peeked out from her head scarf and smiled at Mave. "We call you the undercover goddess."

The little girl stood nearby, entranced with her new toy. Inna looked at her.

"That was a good idea to make them into something children play with," she said. "No one will pay attention."

"Well, the Maryannu did," Mave said. "That's how I got to be game-maker for the Gigante."

They both started at the sound of crashing hooves and the wheels of a heavy cart coming into the marketplace.

"Speak of," Inna said. "Did you conjure him?"

Mave shook her head. She pulled Inna up and shepherded her and the girl behind the table, into her stall, out of the way of the charging chariot-driver. It was the Maryannu with skin as dark as Mave's and her people's, the fellow who appeared to take well to the sun; the Maryannu with bad advice and hands like a woman who had shed tears on Mave's arm while pinning her to the ground. He and his horse-drawn carriage tore through the marketplace, scattering the market goers.

Under the cover of the chariot's rumbling wheels Mave murmured to Inna, "Next new moon, meet with me in the forest above Dia's olive groves."

Inna nodded. She turned her head so that her mouth was at Mave's ear. "Yes," she whispered. "Me and Lat," she continued, her mouth just grazing Mave's lobe.

A pleasant vibration ran from the center of Mave's chest to the bone behind her bud. All women could open their legs to encircle anyone but only the women of the house once known as hieros could hold you there and pass Ssha spirit on. If Inna was one of these former holy prostitutes, somehow she had escaped marriage to a Gigante.

"Lat is my husband," she said, her mouth still close to Mave's ear, lingering on the "s" in husband and drawing it out to a "z."

"And Tear is mine," Mave said. She turned her head and was eye-to-eye with Inna, whose warm breath kissed Mave's lips.

The chariot raced away from them and toward the other side of the market. With a squeeze to Mave's hand, Inna rose, her daughter with her. The streams of people flowed back into the dirt path between the rows of stalls.

Inna clasped her daughter's hand and swung it back and forth. "This is Lat's little girl. I'm mother to her, but not her mother."

Her daughter pulled her hand away to cup and gaze at her chip.

Inna glanced toward the stall with the woman in her jeweled headband and her vials and took Mave's hand. "There's something else I need to tell you."

The chariot was met with cheers from the other Maryannu gathered at the end of the market. The dust settled, for the moment, anyway. The Maryannu were bored.

"Yes?" Mave asked. She liked the feel of Inna's hand in hers.

"Inna," called a young man with a shaggy head of malty brown hair holding the hand of a boy.

Inna waved, and the man and boy stopped at another stall.

"That's Lat," explained Inna. "My partner. I mean, husband. That's his son. Our son, now."

Inna released Mave's hand and led her daughter around the table to the front. Lewi and Levi, Dia's two priests, suddenly appeared at the stall where the woman sold vials of the naptha oil. The small crowd dispersed. The gowns the priests wore were an unforgiving flat black in the bright sun; rivulets of sweat ran down their faces as they gathered up the remaining vials and helped the woman dismantle her stall.

Inna turned back to Mave. "I—" Inna began, then stopped. She bowed her head and puffed up her chest with a long, slow, preparatory breath. She mumbled into her neck bones, "I have to tell you something. There's something you need to know."

A circuit of vibration encircled Mave as though Inna's bones were conduits. Mave grasped her table, steadying herself for the rush of Ssha-like energy; nothing. She looked up. Stars flashed in the brightly lit day. One of the priests held up a vial of the amber liquid in both fists, and the liquid twinkled, as did the red stones in the departing woman's headband as she followed the two priests away from the market.

"Inna," Lat called again, approaching Mave's stall with his boy in hand.

With her head deeply bowed, Inna said, "Next new moon," then turned and walked away with her daughter, to her waiting husband and son.

Two more followers, Mave said in mind-verse to the Ssha. For a moment Mave felt a twinge of what she thought might be the half-and-halfs' energy, a tingle, like a quieter version of the Ssha they served. Tear had once been such a being, lying in the subterranean darkness with the Ssha. Now she was Mave's rock, and her body had become so fully male and solid her consciousness could no longer escape the casing.

The tingly, buzzy feeling in Mave's bones dissipated. Her heart and mind were empty, and she doubted the half-and-halfs had reached out to her; more likely an opportunistic bug had taken a bite of her body. *Eat up*, she thought.

Mave shook the cup and rattled the chips at the passing stream of people. She climbed up on her stool and listened to Tear and her coworkers sing about drunken sailors.

Two more, Mave said again, this time to herself. *Two more, two more*, she hummed along with Tear. The humming vibrated her chest bone, and she sent the vibration down her spine and through her legs, then into the ground beneath her. She imagined it shimmying through dirt, worms and roots and then into deeper darkness. A tiny vibration tickled the bottoms of her feet. "Sh," she said, with her head bowed. Another vibration came up into her feet and traveled up her spine. "Sh," she said again. The vibration shot from the top of her spine into her head. "Sh," sounded in her mind. She closed her eyes, flooded with Ssha energy, relief and happiness.

The back flap of the stall flew open, and in strode Tear. In the past thirteen moon cycles, she'd sprung up in height, and her thighs had grown strong from her treks up and down the mountain and her work on the Gigante cart crew. She'd grown out her hair. Gone were the traditional spikes that had once crested her head in a tiara of triangular points that matched the Lizard People's. Now she tied her hair back as Mave's Uncle Beatt once had, bound in a piece of leather at the nape so that it hung like a horse tail down her back. Her green skin had faded from pine to the dusky olive of the fruit that grew in groves below their cave.

Tear pulled Mave to her in a rough embrace. She bent her head to whisper in Mave's ear, "Any luck?"

Mave breathed in Tear's tangy scent of soot and sweat. "Two more followers," she said into Tear's moist neck.

A cheer went up from behind their tented stall. Tear looked up, pretended surprise, then with a grin pulled the flap securely shut.

"Let's go home," Tear said with a slow push of her hips against Mave's.

They shuttered their rented stall. They paid in Tear's labor and Mave's promise that she would create a new game for the Gigante. They each shouldered a small bag with fruit, barley cakes, and cups for water. Mave looped the ties of her barka bag holding her chips around her wrist. She adjusted her head scarf so the folds hung just above her brow. She followed Tear out of the marketplace.

Dark clouds gathered in the southern sky.

"Hurry," Tear said, and led Mave through the carts in need of repair parked behind the stall. As they wound around the long metal shank of the last cart, Tear stopped. Mave looked up. Tear held her arm and looked around furtively. Then she turned to Mave and pressed herself against her. She kissed Mave and lifted her onto the cart bed, then pulled up Mave's shift. Tear thrust quickly and hard. After she peaked, she rested her forehead briefly on Mave's shoulder then stepped back and pulled on her trousers. Mave sat silently on the cart edge, rocked by waves of pleasure and still longing for more crashes of Tear's body against hers.

"We'd better hurry," Tear said, pulling down Mave's shift and kissing her, "looks like rain."

And just like that, the channel closed. Still wordless, Mave smoothed her shift and adjusted her scarf.

"Let's go," Tear said again.

Mave followed, the rapturous waves in her body slowing into nothing, and the physical memory of Tear's flesh and blood stem shifting to an image of an obelisk of hard darkness. She could not reconcile the two people she had become and considered living with two life streams, one barbarous and shamefully fulfilling, the other dignified and honored in which she kept Ssha knowledge alive. They arrived at the foot of their mountain outside Dia as the sun was setting. The storm clouds had cleared. The sun simmered red on the horizon. They began climbing. Once they cleared the olive groves, they were safe; the Gigante's unrelenting fear of the bones of the dead kept them away from those higher reaches.

While Mave visited Oats and Wonder in the meadow near the cave, Tear bathed using the rainwater they collected in a clay pot on a ledge above and behind the cave. When she was done, she beckoned to Mave. Mave bathed while Tear stood with the horses, drawing her hands in long strokes down their backs. Her broad shoulders jutted like hard wings.

After Mave and Tear ate, they rested their backs against the cool, dark rock and looked at the moon that now hung round and full in the sky. Mave saw the telltale shimmer around the moon and felt the heaviness in her belly, signs the full moon was cresting.

"New moon soon," she said sleepily to Tear. "Inna said she and Lat would join us in the grove."

"That's fine," Tear said.

She put her hand on Mave's thigh. Mave reached down and stroked the folds of skin between Tear's legs. She sought but couldn't find her bud. She moved her hand to Tear's stem. It grew large and hard. Mave stretched her thumb, trying to meet her middle finger, her longest, of the hand encircling Tear's stem. She couldn't.

Tear pinned her arms down and spread her legs apart with her knee, like they'd both seen a Gigante do to a bare-headed woman outside Dia's House of Hor. Love Gigante-style. The theater was elaborate, but the woman from House of Hor played along. The woman had given Mave a little wave from where she lay underneath the Gigante.

Tear's forehead creased in concentration. She clenched her teeth and set her jaw.

Mave lay under Tear, rocking with the rhythm of her thrusting love. Tear collapsed on her, heavy and breathing hard after reaching her peak.

Tear wiped herself with a cloth from a pile they kept near their bedding. She lay next to Mave and stroked her bud, as slippery as a pomegranate seed. Sizzles of pleasure ran up and down Mave's center. The sizzles rose into a peak, and she cried out when the sensation exploded into a melting feeling. Tear rolled over onto her back and fell asleep, and eventually Mave did too, her body and mind quiet, her soul untethered like one of the Gigante small boats, drifting away from the mother ship, leaving safety but free to roam.

The illuminating moon ebbed and diminished. Tear rode the Gigante work cart into Dia, and Mave joined the critters in the mountain-top grove. None of her fellow prey showed themselves to her, but she could feel them, as she could feel Oats and Wonder in their pasture below.

As the moon dwindled to a sickle of light in the sky, Tear stayed in Dia, sleeping in one of the broken-down carts parked behind the marketplace, working on the crew in the day, inhaling the fumes of Gigante fires, stealing olive oil from the presser pans and bread from the market. Mave's body synced with the moon and she bled. When the bleeding stopped, the moon was an ember, a last gasp. That night the critters hidden in the grove grew restless, scratching among the trees and the leaves and sticks on the forest floor.

Mave woke on the morning of the new moon. The sun was high overhead; she had slept late. She had a dream-like memory of the weight of Tear's body on hers. She patted her thighs and stomach; she was naked, and her shift lay crumpled beside her. She turned her head. Tear slept next to her, smelling of wet rock and fire. Mave licked Tear's shoulder. She tasted of salt. Tear woke and smiled at Mave then leaped out of their bedding and pulled Mave with her outside the cave. They foraged for sweet onions and rugula. They placed the vegetables on a clay corver

Tear proudly presented to Mave; she had found it in one of Dia's refuse piles on the southern edge.

They sat just inside the cave and ate. Mave listened for mind-verse from Tear but heard only silence. When they were done, Tear climbed several ledges down to the trench she had dug for their bodily wastes. While she shoveled fresh dirt on the latrine, Mave took Oats and Wonder into the small meadow just beyond their stable. Later Mave made barley cakes with grain, honey, and water, and cooked them in a clay pan over a small fire.

When the sun set, Tear and Mave bathed under the collected rainwater. In the cave, they dressed their hair and bodies with olive oil. Then they made their way to the groves.

The trees' trunks and branches took on the familiar almost-human forms in the new moon darkness. Tear and Mave waited among the trees on the edge of the grove, watching. The creatures coming out in the safety of darkness made soft sounds as they padded along the forest floor. Heavier steps sounded below in the olive groves, around the cave path, into the meadow and up to the grove. Tear and Mave peered out. They could make out two people, and Mave could see the bell shape of the low-hanging head scarf. As the two approached the first trees, the woman pulled back her scarf. It was Inna, with Lat at her side.

Mave introduced them to Tear and beckoned for all three to follow her into the forest. Mave stopped in a spot where the oldest trees grew up and over in a protective canopy. A large stone, flat like a plank, lay on the ground. Mave laid one clay chip on the stone. The chip she chose was the fourth clay chip on which she'd drawn the rabbit dead and staked to form four corners while a bony woman, heavy with child, stood ready with her knife to skin him for dinner. The darkness was so thick that Mave had to grope for Tear's hand next to her and Inna's on her other side. The papery sound of their hands sliding into each other's blended into the soft wind that blew around them.

They stood in their circle, silent. After a time, the pulse of life in Tear's and Inna's hands penetrated Mave's. The pulsing grew to throbbing that slowed like a resting, broken heart. The pauses between beats elongated and stretched. Pulse, pause, pause; pulse, pause, pause. The pauses grew in fullness and crowded into the space between them and the pulses. Mave tumbled into the depth of the pauses, like falling into the trough of a wave or illness, where lulls created their own universe. Mave continued tumbling into this new territory until she rolled into the honeycombed caves of the Ssha. She was like a roaming ghost, consciousness without bodily form. She passed the round hall with the half-and-halfs in their slumber.

"Sister Aleph, farther," came a raspy voice, one that existed in a space between waking and slumber, the realm of the Goddess, the space between human and divine time. Mave thought of the female Ssha who had shown her kindness that time in their caves. She had abandoned Ssha mind-verse and spoken to Mave using her voice, not an easy effort for a Ssha.

Mave spirited through the dark halls. Her consciousness entered a room like a wisp of smoke. The walls thrummed with vibrations. Again she thought of the kind, giant lizard and her croaky, gentle voice. A purr seemed to emanate from a spot low on the wall. Mave drifted closer. She could only see shades of black and white. A haze gathered in front of this particular spot on the wall. As she watched, it took shape. The image of the kind, giant Ssha formed, her scaled belly, her head crested with a tiara of three triangular points, and the slow-blinking slits of her eyes. The last time they had been in each other's presence she rose above Mave, her belly at Mave's eye level. Now in her spirit essence form she seemed more compact. They faced each other, eye to eye.

There were no words, either spoken or exchanged in mindverse. There was only vibration thrumming through Mave.

With a whoosh, Mave was back in the circle. She shook with Ssha vibrations. Tear and Inna gripped her hands. Mave sent the tremors from her hands to theirs, and in turn to Lat who stood between them on the other side of the circle. Mave's feet were numb. She kept still in the soft night with the tree branches canopied overhead and fed all she had taken in from the Ssha to Tear, Inna, and Lat.

When the vibrations had subsided from all of them and slid in their circuit back to the Ssha, they let go of each other's hands. The soft wind had stilled, preparing for dawn, the night of the new moon in its last moment of deep quiet before the next sun cycle began. Tears sprang to Mave's eyes. *Later*, she said to her most inner self; *you can cry later*. They only had a little while before Inna and Lat must return to Apollonoulous, a half-day's walk.

The four of them sat on the edge of the grove, watching the horizon turn from inky dark to a purplish blue. The sun cast a glow from where it lurked below the horizon. Mave put the clay chip in the barka bag with the others and opened a cloth with barley cakes. She passed them around.

"What do we do with what you've given us?" Lat asked, then took a bite of a barley cake.

Inna munched her cake and looked at Mave expectantly. Tear finished one of the sweet bricks and reached for another.

"I think the vibrations ground you and connect you to the Ssha," Mave said. "Eventually you'll be able connect directly to them. With that connection, you can explore realms without the need of your physical body." Mave wasn't exactly sure if this was right. She trusted that the words coming out of her mouth originated from her Ssha friends deep below.

Inna and Lat nodded.

Inna tilted the clay jug back and drank a draught of water. "The Gigante priests have asked the women formerly of hieros house to add a new consort to our Queen the Goddess," she said. "The Gigante want to give her a king."

"What did the women say?" Mave asked.

Inna and Lat exchanged a glance, and both smiled.

"We said yes," Inna said.

"You're of hieros house," Mave said, confirming, not asking.

"I was, when there was a hieros house. Everything changed once Poulx married Thras. Mave, I have to tell you something."

Lat interrupted. "The women offered a trade: if the Gigante would give them two of their horse-drawn chariots and driving lessons from the Maryannu warriors, they would give the Goddess a king of the Gigante's choosing."

Tear made a croaking sound. Mave, Inna, and Lat all turned to her. Tear coughed and crumbs from the barley cake shot out of her mouth. Mave patted her back. Inna looked forlornly at the rising sun.

"What is this king's name?" Mave asked, turning back to Lat, keeping her hand on Tear's warm back.

"Dyaus Pitar," said Lat. "God Father."

Inna continued to stare at the horizon.

God Father, Mave said to herself. *Godfather*.

"They also agreed to change our holy writings to say Dyaus Pitar let Hera reign and married her to allow her this," Lat said.

"Hera?" Mave asked.

"That's what they're calling the Goddess," Inna said. "They've split her up into two: Hera and another called Gaia. Hera is the king's wife, and Gaia is mother earth." She paused. "Our women of hieros house also agreed to teach the Gigante how to write in our language."

"How have they been writing their records?" Mave asked.

"They have no real records," Inna said. "But soon they will, including the new stories of the king marrying the Goddess to rescue her from darkness and bringing her to live in his kingdom of light."

Mave had heard this before. Light was good, dark was bad. Undergrounds, new moon nights, their island skin—all these dusky things were changing from revered to despised.

The horizon smoldered with the sun's predictable light. Mave preferred the moon, her coolness and her erratic rhythm. She might rise low in the sky one night and high the next. And in that cadence she waxed and waned. Mave's body joined the moon in her tempo, swelling like an ocean wave then breaking and flowing into shore. Any man, even a Gigante, could step into the wrap of a woman's legs and participate in that pattern. But the Gigante didn't want collaboration.

Inna donned her scarf. She secured it by looping a length of twisted fabric around her head and tying the ends in a knot just above her ear. She tugged the tassel of tufted threads, making them dance, and pulled a face at Lat, raising her brows, crossing her eyes and smiling as goofily as Turnip might, her lips pulled back like a braying donkey.

Mave watched. What hope was there if someone like Inna, a believer in the Goddess and darkness, could so easily adapt to the changes the Gigante were bringing, even finding humor in them?

"Til next month," Inna said, and Lat nodded. They rose.

"You'll come?" Mave asked.

Inna's toothy smile faded. "Of course," she said.

"Come, woman," Lat said, and the two of them laughed as they headed out of the grove.

Mave sat quietly with Tear as they listened to Inna and Lat

tromp down through the olive trees. A circuit of throbbing ran from the Ssha up to Mave, across to Tear, back to Mave and down again to the Ssha.

As Tear had that morning, she pulled Mave to standing. She cupped Mave's face and stared into her eyes, then closed hers. The pulse of the life in her hands warmed the bones of Mave's jaw, returning her fully to the waking realm. Tear's words slipped into her mind: *Rest, now.*

Together they walked back to their cave. Mave stopped to speak to Oats and Wonder where they stood outside their shelter munching grass. They whinnied when they saw her. She stood between them and let them nuzzle her neck and the crook of her arms. Both snuffled her hands hopefully. She mimed "nothing," showing her empty palms. Oats nosed her pocket while Wonder watched. Mave smiled, brought out the two remaining barley cakes and fed one to each.

Inside, Tear had already laid down on the nest of blankets at the back of the cave. Mave joined her. Tear pressed up against the length of her body. Mave opened her arms and Tear, her rock, rolled onto her, her muscled body laying heavily on Mave's, a blanket of stone.

11
Skeleton Shrine

THE TREES IN THE GROVE called Mave back but her fate lay in town, she was sure. She pulled down her head scarf to hide her glee as she and Tear crossed the plain in the pre-dawn and approached Dia, enveloped in its sooty haze. Mave had done her part and connected to the Ssha. She and Tear would find Turnip, and Mave would tell him her good news; beyond that, she owed him nothing. The weight of the gold quartz rocks in Mave's pockets told her change was near. At day's end, she'd reveal her handful of surprise to Tear: enough Gigante money to quit her job and return to the groves with Mave, never again to ride the work cart into Dia.

Tear put an ashy hand on Mave's arm. "Look," she said.

Mave lifted the rim of her scarf. Rays of the rising sun shot through the skeleton shrine, striping the plain. The structure lorded over the cozy, round pods of heiros house, former hovels of holy women, now places to pay for sex. A spire pointed to the sky where the Gigante god lived.

Barks and shouts came from beyond the structure, near the stables, where the Maryannu argued and hitched their horses to the chariots. One of the helmeted warriors punched his comrade then his horse. Mave pulled her scarf back down and let Tear lead her, sightless, into Dia, the Maryannu's grumbling growing behind them.

In the marketplace, only a few of Dia's citizens were about, men in their Gigante-like trousers held up with strands of hemp setting up their stalls.

Turnip pranced up to Tear and Mave. He shook his head like a dog coming out of the water, and the bells on the end of the crimson ribbons tinkled. He pawed the air with his imaginary hooves.

"I have news," Turnip said and grinned his lunatic's smile.

"So does Mave," said Tear, setting her in front of Turnip.

Mave edged her head scarf back.

"Mave," Turnip said, peering at her from under the cloth edge, "I'm so happy to see you." He twirled away and pretended to trip then lurched back toward Mave. Tear's strong arms caught him, and while Tear held him he whispered, "Tomorrow the Gigante will give us the chance to join our beliefs to theirs."

Both Tear and Mave helped Turnip right himself. Tear slapped him on the back, and Mave patted his arm.

"I have news," Mave said.

Turnip continued as though he hadn't heard her. "After each service, the priests revise the laws they're writing. They watch the people for their reactions first."

The Maryannu in their chariots set out toward the market, lashing their horses. Turnip gestured to a bench, and they sat down. Tear hovered protectively, as though she expected someone might spirit Mave away.

"You'll come, won't you, to the service tomorrow, outside the shrine?" Turnip asked. "It starts at sunrise."

"Turnip," Mave said. "I made connection with the Ssha." She shook her head, the sensation of achievement tinkling like falling crystals in her head. "It's not like before where we could exchange words. But it's vibration, strong and coursing. It's a good first step."

Turnip patted her hand. "We may not need the Ssha," he said. "The Gigante want to blend our two religions. Maybe that's a better way. We wouldn't be so dependent on the Ssha then. The Gigante will find a place for our Goddess in their beliefs!"

Mave tilted her head to look at Turnip then at Tear who scanned the marketplace as the Maryannu thundered away from Dia in races with each other on the plain.

Mave had no words. The trees had taken those out of her and in their place created empty grooves, channels to conduct Ssha energy. Her hands grew warm. "Here," she said, placing her hands on Turnip's arm, thumbs touching. "That's Ssha power."

He sat quietly for a few moments. "I'd forgotten how gentle it is," he said, patting Mave's hands. "Maybe too gentle for these new times?"

Mave looked south at the spire that rose like a spine and the dust cloud the Maryannu's chariots stirred up in their rumbling race as they skirted the market.

"Tomorrow we have a real chance at affecting Gigante rule," Turnip said. "We need as many as possible to attend the service. We can influence the rules they are making. Don't you see? This would be even better than reconnecting with Ssha energy."

Tear swooped toward Turnip. "We'll be there," Tear hissed. "Maryannu," she said, and yanked Mave up. Tear pulled her close and wedged them both behind the bench.

Turnip bobbed his head, curtsied, and ran off into the market.

A single Maryannu and his horse-drawn chariot barreled into the marketplace while the other Maryannu gathered at the northern end and shouted and cheered. The chariot's sides rose up to the Maryannu's waist. The Maryannu wore a metal face mask protecting his forehead, nose and jaw. His skin was surprisingly dark. Anyone of stature now had light skin. The Gigante god was very clear about this—light was good, dark was bad.

The chariot drew close to where Tear and Mave stood huddled. The driver pulled up on the horse's reins, and he clattered to a stop in front of them. A stripe of light shone on the Maryannu's face. The upper lip curled, as though smelling a latrine, and the eyes were barely open, squinting like a snake. The gaze fastened on Mave. For a second the eyes brightened and danced, recalling the look of only one in Mave's life, a look she had not seen since Anta held her in her arms and offered her up: her mother's. Mave had not seen her since that day she encountered her disguised as a hobbled old woman in the rubble of the Gigante invasion. She'd gone from old woman to male warrior and joined the elite Maryannu. As the cart passed Tear and Mave, her mother's gaze shifted from her to Tear. Mave knew that look; she was appraising Tear.

Mave's Maryannu mother snapped her whip against the horse's tender neck. Mave cringed. The horse whinnied and reared up, and the people in the growing crowd jumped as though they too had been whipped. The chariot rumbled away, drawn by the frightened, galloping horse.

Her mother, the masquerading Maryannu, steered the horse and chariot out of the market and away from her comrades. Clouds of dust rose up behind her. She was heading to the edge of the town, where the Gigante were building their shrine. The spire pointed the way.

Mave looked sideways at Tear. Tear's shoulders drooped. She curved into herself, around the bones that guarded her heart. She resembled the silent, obedient half-and-half Mave had first met. When Tear served the Ssha, she had kept her individual abilities tightly furled, like a rock rose on a cool winter morning. Working among the Gigante had allowed her to expand in a way Ssha and Goddess spirit had not. Now, with the reappearance of Mave's mother, Tear folded up.

Lines etched along Tear's brow and cheeks, and the olive darkness under her eyes had a greyish tint. Mave ran her thumb along Tear's brow then down her cheek and along her jaw.

"Let's go home," Mave said to her.

The gold quartz weighed like a promise in her pockets; she would sell the rocks tomorrow after the Gigante service. Fate could wait a day.

When they reached their cave and had eaten and seen to the horses, Mave lay down next to Tear in their nest of blankets. She couldn't bear to see her so reduced. She stroked her stem then play-acted reticence. Tear growled and parted Mave's knees. Mave feigned resistance, saying "No, no," fighting Tear off. She play-acted giving in, swooning in Tear's arms, and Tear peaked in a flurry of abandonment.

While Tear slept, Mave sat at the front of their cave. The moon was halfway toward full and curved above Dia.

Mother, Mave called in mind-verse. She heard a rustling in the bushes. In the moon's light a transparent, four-footed creature emerged. It was the size of a large cat but had a long, sinewy body and horns instead of ears.

"Mother?" Mave asked the creature.

The cat-like being advanced toward Mave. It didn't seem to see her. Mave could see through its furry body. Almost on top of Mave, it met her gaze. Startled, it fluttered its long eyelashes as it blinked at Mave, then faded into nothingness.

Definitely not my mother, thought Mave. Had her mother mastered the ability to assume other forms and appear and disappear at will, she would have stayed to tell Mave about it.

Mave looked out over the plains and at Dia in the smoky dark. If Turnip was right, tomorrow they would weave their ways and beliefs with the Gigante's. All would have a voice. In Dia's old ways, only a select few had a voice. Perhaps Dia's ways had become too restrictive. Mave expected to feel happiness and relief at Turnip's prediction about tomorrow, but felt nothing. Her role seemed no longer to be needed. Like her little horned friend, she could disappear into nothingness.

The next morning Tear and Mave rose while the sky was still dark. Tear made her way down to their vegetable patch, and Mave spent time with Oats and Wonder.

"How are my dears?" she asked both horses as she stood between them and stroked their sides. Both leaned their warm flanks against her. They nickered, the gentle rolling whinny deep in their throats while nuzzling her with their noses. Mave had no barley cakes, only grass she'd gathered by the fistful and stuck in her pockets. They played their game where Mave stood before them with wide eyes and open, empty hands, and both dug in her pockets for the treats they knew lay inside.

As long as the horses played her game she knew life held them there with her.

Tear and Mave ate the raw tubers Tear had dug up. Tear pulled on her tan Gigante trousers, and Mave oiled her fingers and ran them through her hair. When the curls coiled along her shoulders and back, she lay the tan square of cloth on her head with the edge hanging over her forehead, just above the eyebrows. She tied a slender strip of cloth around her head to secure the larger piece of fabric. When Tear was ready, they paused at the entrance to their cave. They raised their arms to the sun that crested the horizon and felt the warmth that would soon flood the day.

They reached Dia as the sky grew pink at the horizon. They made their way to the edge of town where the skeleton shrine stood. They joined others on their way, the women all wearing head scarves like Mave's, allowing them a square of sight at their feet.

Tear pulled Mave along as she gazed down at the dirt road. Mave was happy to let go of what she'd thought was her destiny. She let her mind relax, something she hadn't been able to do for a long time. She daydreamed as she had once as a girl, before the Gigante, when she was the daughter of star counsel. "Sh," she whispered quietly, a shortening of a call to the Ssha, playing that game of her youth in which she talked in her mind with the Lizard People. Uttering "sh" could not get her in trouble. The Gigante liked it when women shushed themselves. Tear glanced quickly back at Mave and grimly smiled.

Mave continued her daydreaming and soft whispering of "Sh." She imagined the sound of her soft shush traveling down inside the dirt to the crystalline roof of the Ssha's caves where they lay in suspended sleep. She pictured the sound traveling through the halls until it reached the room where the giant lizards lay. She let it snake its way into the room and nose around until it found her kind Ssha friend just behind the membrane wall.

Do you have a name? Mave asked her imaginary friend lying still.

Sister Ssha, she heard.

In Mave's mind's eye, Sister Ssha's scaled eyes popped open. She stared blindly up, her pupils dark diamond shapes.

Sleep, sleep, Mave crooned to her gentle lizard friend. Mave imagined Sister Ssha's eyes closing to slits. Instead, Sister Ssha sat up.

Frantic, Mave pulled on Tear's arm. "I think I've done something terrible," she said.

Tear turned. She had the same look in her eyes as Mave's gentle giant lizard, vacant, under another's control. Tear abruptly shifted course and pushed against the flow of the crowd, making her way with Mave in tow out of town and in the direction of old Ssha mountain.

Turnip appeared at Mave's side, quickly peeking under her head scarf. Turnip pried her arm from Tear's grasp and tucked it inside the crook of his arm. Tear did not turn and continued her advancement toward Ssha mountain. Turnip smiled brightly and turned Mave around so that the two of them were caught up in the flow of people heading toward the skeleton shrine.

Turnip was strong. Pull as Mave might, she could not loosen her arm from his grasp.

Tear, Tear, Mave cried in mind-verse. There was no reassuring hum of an answer. There was only emptiness.

Turnip pulled Mave into the crowd of standing people. All eyes were on the raised platform of the skeleton shrine. The sun began to crest the horizon through bloody streaks in the sky. A squadron of Maryannu and their horse-drawn chariots rolled up and stopped in protective ranks on either side of Mave and Turnip. Mave scanned up and down the line, one side, then the other. She found the glinting pair of eyes hidden within the frame of a face shield; Audria and her chariot stood at the end of the line.

The Gigante priest Lewi strode to the center of the raised platform. The citizens of Dia pushed forward.

"We will bring you out of darkness," Lewi called out just as the sun rose above the horizon, the rays shining on his white face and well-oiled light brown hair.

Lewi was not as tall as the Gigante but even so rose at least two heads above Mave and the people around her. He wore a long black robe and over it the familiar shawl of crimson and violet sashes. The fabric looked soft and shiny in the rays of the rising sun.

The crowd grew quiet. Mave's stomach churned. She'd wakened a Ssha. Mave was not supposed to have that ability; it lay only among the Ssha and perhaps the worms, their familiars.

Mave heard a rustling at the back of the crowd. Lewi pitched forward and peered in that direction. Then he settled back on the soles of his feet. A grim smile spread across his face.

"We will save you from the fallen angel, who lives in darkness, hiding from God," Lewis said. "He whispers into the ears of women and makes them disobedient. He causes men to listen to those wicked women. If you follow him, you will spend the afterlife in his fiery darkness."

Mave shook her head, struggling to make sense of what he was saying. On the one hand, the fallen angel lived in darkness, but on the other kept fires burning for the humans who would join him after death.

"Behold God's fallen angel," the priest shouted and pointed toward the back of the crowd.

Everyone turned. Many people cried out and fell to the ground, burying their faces in their arms. Turnip and Mave remained standing along with a few others. Tear advanced up the aisle with Sister Ssha in tow, pulling her along with a rope knotted around her neck. She rose twice as high as any of them, several heads above the priest, as tall, it seemed, as one of the Gigante. Sister Ssha no longer had the vacant stare she'd had in Mave's vision; instead she appeared bewildered. She stumbled on her scaled, three-toed feet, the talons raking through the dirt.

Audria sprang into action. In her Maryannu disguise, she

snapped her whip against her horse's flank, her metal face mask glinting in the sun now blazing low in the sky. The horse wheeled around, pulling Audria in her chariot, and they charged toward Tear and Sister Ssha.

Audria pulled up her horse abruptly in front of them. She lassoed both Tear and Sister Ssha with her whip and reeled them in. She yanked them against her chariot, and they stood facing the crowd. Through her metal face mask Audria looked expectantly toward the platform where the other priest, Levi, had joined Lewi.

A Gigante lumbered up the steps and joined the two priests, positioning himself between them. The Gigante's white face reddened in the sun's bright rays. Lewi and Levi flanked him, standing as tall as his armpit, and waited.

Moans came from the people lying face-down in the dirt.

The Gigante called out, "We'll protect you. Don't fear. You, Maryannu," he shouted at Audria, "Cover the heads of the serpent and the drudge so no one need look at them, then bring them to the council chambers."

12

Zet Rises

AUDRIA TETHERED THE REINS OF her horse to a hook on the side of her chariot. In her Maryannu garb, she bent below into her chariot then rose back up with woven hemp bags in her hands. She jumped out of the chariot in her sandals with leather strings that wound up her stout, muscular calves. She shoved Sister Ssha and Tear into the chariot, then threw one hemp bag over the Ssha's head and another over Tear's. Audria wheeled the cart around. The force of the sharp turn threw Sister Ssha down, and Tear beside her. Off they flew, Audria whipping the horse and Sister Ssha and Tear bouncing around in the small cab of the chariot. Even sitting and shrouded in a hemp sack, Sister Ssha rose up as tall as Audria. One scaled claw gripped the edge of the cart as they sped away.

Mave turned back toward the raised platform where the two priests and the Gigante stood. Lewi and Levi snuck sideways looks at each other as though to say, "Now what?"

"It's safe now," called out the Gigante standing between them. "You can rise up."

The people on the ground unfolded from their crouches and stood and faced the raised platform. Murmurings arose among the people.

"God Father will always protect you," the Gigante said. He looked at the two priests on either side of him and mimed "Go ahead" with a little sweeping gesture.

Lewi stepped forward. "If you follow God Father's words and ways, then he will protect you."

The Gigante nodded approvingly. Lewi puffed up his chest. Levi glowered.

"Go now," the Gigante said, "and tell everyone you meet about what happened today." The murmuring crowd dispersed.

Turnip rose up on his tiptoes beside Mave, bouncing up and down, a wide, silly grin plastered across his face.

He whispered, "I'm sorry, Mavealeph. This isn't at all what I was expecting. I'm not sure what to do or think."

Confusion, hallmark of the Gigante, thought Mave. "Did you recognize my mother?" Mave asked quietly as the people drifted out of the skeleton shrine.

He nodded. "I can guess where in the council chambers she's taken the Ssha and Tear. I can take you there," he said through his silly smile.

In this new world to be stupid was a kind of currency, gaining a person entrance to palaces of power. Another option was to act as a slave or as a captive, but then you had to do double duty, always on the lookout for surprising your captor and bursting out of your slave bonds. Yet another option was to be something in between—a well-behaved woman. Since she couldn't go wrong with this option, Mave adopted the appropriate manner for a woman who knows her place. She adjusted her head scarf to frame her face in an enclosure that allowed her to peer through a tunnel, bowed her head, and shuffled alongside the prancing Turnip who led them to the council chambers.

The building that housed the Gigante along with the Executrix and Turnip sat on the edge of town. The sun cast its harsh glare on the barren ground surrounding the Gigante compound. Turnip led Mave past a vegetable garden on the outskirts of the compound where a woman knelt on her hands and knees pulling weeds. They wound around the water well and the pen holding the Executrix' pigs. Chickens scratched and pecked the ground near a bloody table where the animals were slaughtered. A boy with blackened cheeks and singed hair stoked the fire of an iron forge.

Turnip hopped up to the back door, opened it, and Mave followed him into the kitchen with her head bowed. A pair of bedraggled boys walked a tiny circle around an upright beam. They pushed a bar driven through the beam which turned a spit of cooking meat the size of a calf. A scowling woman stirred a pot. She glanced up, then looked back at her boiling pot. The boys did not look up.

Turnip led Mave out of the kitchen and through a dark hall, emerging into the hub of the main building. He paused. The unmistakable voice of the Executrix, her sharp, raspy tones, cut the air.

"…in the questioning room," she said. "We'll keep them there until we know what we'll do with them. We've got one of the Maryannu guarding them."

Turnip looked at Mave then cocked his head in the direction of another hallway branching off the main area.

They crept down the hall. They passed a room where Mave saw the backs of the two priests from the platform that morning,

Lewi and Levi. They were bent over a length of tightly woven fiber and each held quill poised over a small bowl of dark liquid.

"Should the serpent have a name?" asked Levi. "Or should we just call it 'serpent?'"

Lewi tapped a finger on their worktable. "Apollyon," he said. "Destroyer."

"Too hard to say," Levi said. "Ua Zit? The snake. Also a name for their goddess. Or Zet. Same thing. Zet is easier to say."

Lewi nodded. "All right," he said. "Zet."

Mave and Turnip moved noiselessly past their door and went down stone steps to a lower level. In the dim light that filtered in through the stair well, Mave saw a heavy wooden door. Turnip knocked once, paused, then rapped again, two sharp strikes. Slowly he pulled the door open, and they slipped inside.

In front of them was a sort of tableau, a Maryannu holding a knife to the throat of Sister Ssha while the Maryannu's sandaled foot, broad as a brick, pinned Tear down at the neck.

The Maryannu turned. With a sigh of relief, the Maryannu released both the Ssha and Tear, then pulled off the metal face grill.

"Mavealph!" whispered Mave's mother, coming toward her with open arms.

Audria embraced her. Mave stood stiffly. She endured her mother's strong squeeze of a hug, subdued by the constriction.

"Sister Ssha," Mave said, her voice muffled by her mother's shoulder pressing into her face, "and Tear. Can I speak to them?"

"Of course!" Audria said, releasing Mave from her hold.

Mave sat down next to Tear who put her arm around Mave. Her touch was gentle, like the old Tear, as though she had resumed her original half-and-half nature.

Mave faced her Ssha friend. Her wise eyes took Mave in, and she slowly opened and closed her scaled eyelids. She tilted her head with its tiara of three points.

Mind-verse? Mave heard in her mind.

Sister Ssha nodded. *We had to do it*, Sister Ssha said, *to bring us all together. Were you surprised by your ability to wake me?*

Mave nodded.

Our great need called it out of you, she said.

Sister Ssha leaned her back against the wall where she sat. Even sitting she rose twice as high as Mave. Mave looked up at her as she closed the slits of her eyes. For a few moments there was only a kind of purring in Mave's mind.

Sister Ssha opened her eyes. *No Ssha has been above ground for many, many years*, she said. *I'd forgotten how bright and loud it is up here. The Gigante add even more noise. No one can hear our mind-verse, not even the women once of hieros house. We couldn't reach anyone. Except you, of course.*

But there are others, Mave implored Sister Ssha in her mind. *I'm not the only average human who can moisovo. Turnip, someone from Dia, said he and others have been trying to send information to you and the other Ssha using mind-verse.*

Sister Ssha instinctively recoiled, pulling back from Mave. *Unless we train or initiate a human, their thoughts can never reach us*, she said. *Humans don't naturally communicate this way with us.*

Does this mean above-ground humans can't help by sending you messages in the underground?

Their mass of thoughts would crush our minds.

Both Mave and Sister Ssha sat silently for a few moments.

For now it's a select few, said Sister Ssha in Mave's mind. *We lost the ability to reach Tear soon after the Gigante overran Dia. Living outside our underground home, she took on new characteristics that made it harder to reach her.*

Tear looked at Mave then hung her head.

She'll return to the caves, Sister Ssha said.

Mave's stomach dropped. "No," she said, forgetting mind-verse and speaking aloud. "Tear is all I have. I have no one else."

Her reptile friend looked questioningly at her.

Please, Mave said in mind-verse, imagining her words singing through the air into Sister Ssha's lizard brain, *I'm able to live because I have Tear at my side.*

Mave's mother dropped on one knee beside her. *You're a grown woman now*, came her words into Mave's mind. Audria put her arm around Mave and squeezed her shoulders. *Time to meet your fate. The rest of us already have. Join us!*

Mave turned back to Sister Ssha. One scaly eyelid drooped, swollen from Audria's blow before the mad rush in her chariot. Tendrils of Sister Ssha's exhaustion reached toward her.

You are our gateway, Sister Ssha said in mind-verse to Mave. *We need you when we try to reach beyond our time and transform others. We don't understand it; we just know we need it. We felt our energy move through you and into the others at the last new moon ritual. Over time, we hope can find more portals so it isn't just you. But for now, it is.*

Mave squeezed her eyes shut. *I won't*, she said in her mind. She stood up abruptly. Tear, Sister Ssha, and Audria all stared at her.

I'm leaving, Mave said, turning and moving toward the door where Turnip stood guard.

"Out of the way," she said to Turnip who was too surprised to do anything but what Mave commanded.

Mave ran down the hall, past Lewi and Levi bent over their scribing, through the main area and the hall leading into the kitchen and out the door. She ran past the pig lot and the horse stable and toward the western edge of Dia. She kept running across the plains, her lungs burning, and, eventually, up through the brush which tore at her legs then the olive groves and, finally, their cave. Now Mave's cave.

She stood at the cave entrance and looked out over the plain in the day's dying light. *I'm done being of service*, she decided. *I'll live out my days with Oats and Wonder. We can move to Apollonoulous and join Inna and Lat.*

Her hands closed over the gold quartz in her pockets, and she made her final vow: *My mother and my former Ssha friend or should I say Zet can both go to the evil darkness the Gigante priests have invented. I will close my heart to them and to Tear so none of them can ever reach me again.*

13
Eclipse Season

THAT NIGHT MAVE SLEPT WITH Oats and Wonder in their stall, starlight winking through the branches of the canopy. Oats took first watch while Mave and Wonder slept. When morning dawned and Mave woke, the horses had traded places: Oats lay next to her, and Wonder stood at the ready.

Mave walked with Oats and Wonder to a spot on the ridge where sweet hay grew. Heavy clouds obscured the sun's light. Soon the sun and moon would take turns disappearing, finding respite in darkness before the work of planting, and, later, during harvest. While the horses munched the grass, Mave pulled out fistfuls and chewed on several slender blades. She rose and walked through the grass to where the trees began. She stepped into the shade of the grove. Her hunt for the brown-capped mushrooms took her deeper in. She collected a handful from the base of several trees and returned to the edge of the grove.

She sat under the shade of a tree and ate the mushrooms. Oats and Wonder chewed grass, and Mave drowsed then fell into a half-sleep where she watched a young woman lying down in a tall structure like the Gigante's shrine but smaller, and she was alone inside it. The sun shone in a slant through an opening that was clear and had a hard surface. The young woman lay on a blanket that was placed perfectly even all around her. It was more like a carpet of grass in its symmetry. Mave fell into the young woman's mind and the vision unfolded. A man like the Gigante but with brown instead of white hair battled a Ssha. He and the giant reptile fought only with their bodies, swinging fists and wrestling each other to the ground. The man won. The Ssha expired on a hump of ground. Then his body and its iridescent scales of green and blue-black melted into the mound and only unfamiliar white markings remained—one long white stripe crossed at the top with a short white bar. This was the winner's mark. Then the young woman's vision shifted. She stood in a busy marketplace but without the familiar wood-slatted stalls, dirt roads, and view of trees in the distance. This place was enclosed by walls that looked hard; they had none of the softness of the clay walls of the old Dia or the cool rock of Mave's cave. These walls were uniform, like the carpet or blanket the young woman lay on. As the young woman watched all the people moving about, going in and out of the enclosed market stalls, a young man with brown hair approached her and said, "Get to know the lizard men of revelations; we need more of their kind."

With that, Mave woke, abruptly pulled back into her own time.

"Back into my own time," Mave repeated to herself, aloud, words she had never strung together in a sentence. She held tightly to the gold quartz in her pockets, as though their rocky souls could penetrate her bones and root her to the dirt. So much for closing herself off to the Ssha and what they decided they needed her to do.

The sun set in a pink glow behind the gray clouds. A soft, diffuse red light bathed the meadow, Oats, and Wonder as well as the tips of the grass they ate. Mave felt drowsy from the mushrooms and floated somewhere between sleep and waking. The anger and sadness were easier to bear in such a state.

For the next few weeks, Mave ate a handful of the brown-capped mushrooms on waking. The mornings had grown misty and so she stayed inside the cave, sitting on a blanket and resting her back against the wall, sitting just far enough in so the light could not touch her but she could still see out and hear Oats' and Wonders' gentle rumblings and their hooves moving through the grass. As the mushrooms took effect, she noticed her hands: they were draining of color. So were her arms, legs, and feet. All of her grew fainter. For a moment she thought she saw her horned friend. Then Mave's eyelids grew heavy and they shut, and she was again the witness to the young woman in the first vision.

The young woman was in a similar structure as previously, with its hard walls and carpet of blanket. She lay asleep, as before, but Mave sensed her mind awake and alert, scanning her surroundings, seeking and open, it seemed to Mave, to mind-verse. However, her mind was sharply divided between this openness and another part that shook with fear. Mave tried to comfort her, to assure her there was nothing to fear about mind-verse. A part of her would leave the safe container of her body, Mave explained mind to mind, and roam her realm. She must already be doing so, Mave reasoned, if she had connected with Mave. But Mave's soothing messages could not reach past the young woman's fear. Mave's heart went out to her, and she stopped trying to convince the young woman. Mave remembered only too well the immobilizing fear border time had once evoked in her.

She also remembered how Anta's sweet smells of bergamot and warm skin had comforted her. Mave willed her physical body into the young woman's time. But the best she could do was a mist that grew thicker until it resembled a bald and naked child, nodding at the young woman. Instead of Mave's presence soothing the young woman, it terrified her. She sat up straight on the raised platform on which she slept, breathing hard. She held her hand over her heart as though to quiet it and tried to calm her ragged breath. She put her hand on the neck of what looked like a vase on a smaller raised platform next to her bed, and suddenly a light flared at the top of the vase. In surprise, Mave fell out of the slender thread of connection they had, and was sucked backward out of the young woman's time.

Mave spent her days and nights like this for the next few weeks. Inna and Lat came to visit as the moon grew full.

"Mavealeph?" Inna called from the cave entrance. Both she and Lat peered in.

"I'm here," Mave said, coming to stand in front of them at the cave entrance, where the waxing moon shone its silvery light.

"I can barely see you," Lat said.

Mave shook her head, though Lat likely couldn't see her. "These realms the Ssha are sending me to—they're changing me into something else."

Lat shrunk back. Inna stepped closer, groped for Mave's hand, and, when she found it, held it.

Mave told them what had happened in Dia, the Gigante priests uniting the people in fear against the Ssha, and Sister Ssha taking Tear back to the caves and closing them off.

"We heard," Inna said. "Our hieros house women—" She stopped herself. "Our Council of Businesswomen said the

Gigante revealed the true nature of the Ssha and saved everyone from their evil."

"That's what happened," Mave said, "but I wouldn't say their words were true. No matter," she continued. "I'm here alone now."

"Come with us to Apollonoulous," Inna said, taking both of Mave's hands into hers and holding them tightly.

"I'll be fine for now," Mave said. "As mad as I am at the Ssha for all this, I'm curious about what they're having me do, moving back and forth in time. I want to see where these nightly journeys are taking me." She paused and pulled out several gold quartz rocks from her pockets. "Can you get me naphtha oil with this?" Mave asked, handing Inna the rocks. "I saw a woman selling vials of the oil at your marketplace."

Inna dropped to her knees. She buried her face in her hands. "That was Korinsia," she said, "one of my former hieros house sisters. Mave," Inna raised her head, "it's my fault the Gigante overran Dia. I discovered the oil they use for their explosions and fires."

Mave lowered herself to sitting next to Inna. Lat paced the walkway along the caves.

"Who makes the money when the women sell the naphtha oil?" Mave asked Inna.

Inna wiped the tears off her face with the back of her hand. "The businesswomen of Apollonoulous. But we give a portion of it to the Gigante for bringing us the peat." Inna looked down, forlorn and afraid that the truth would cost her Mave's friendship.

Mave cupped her hands around Inna's. "If you hadn't figured out how to extract the oil, somebody else would have," she said, pressing her forehead to Inna's. "If you hadn't given it to the Gigante, they would have taken it from you."

Mave kissed Inna's cheek. They sat in the cool night air for a little while longer, then Inna rose and joined Lat on the trail. With a wave, they began the journey back to Apollonoulous.

Another moon cycle passed. Mave's body continued to grow lighter until she could almost see through her limbs. She'd lost interest in her morning mushrooms and nibbled on grasses with Oats and Wonder. Her belly grew heavy and she knew she would bleed soon. Inna and Lat appeared at the cave entrance. They called Mave's name; she sat silently far back in the cave. She was drowsy from a night of witnessing the young woman.

After Inna and Lat had gone, Mave went to the entrance. Her two friends had left purple flowers and several willow branches. They had also left one small vial of naphtha oil. Mave clasped the amber glass and let the flowers and branches tipped in silvery white lay at the cave entrance.

Her blood flowed then ebbed, and Mave buried the leaves she had sat on to catch the blood. Inna and Lat again made their way to her cave. They stood before the entrance as though at a portal and left bread and a jug of wine. As soon as they left, Mave brought the bread and wine inside and ate and drank. These were the hardest moments, which brought on thoughts of Tear, their time together and what they had shared. Mave resolved to drink from the stream that ran into the pasture and eat grass with the horses.

The moon made its way to the darkness of a new moon. The darker nights drew more silent visitors to Mave's cave. They left gifts of flowers, branches and, once, honey.

Mave dreamed of dying. This was good news. It meant the first eclipse of the season was coming, when the sun would fall into darkness, mimicking the moon. Mave reversed her usual rhythm. She slept during the day and rose with the moon. She took in the moon's light as she had once taken in the sun's.

A few days before the new moon, when only a thin horn of light hung in the sky, Mave joined Oats and Wonder in the meadow. It was just after nightfall and the horses' manes shone pearly gray.

Mave sat with her back against a tree just inside the grove, watching the horses. If her sense was right, the next new moon would be one of great changes in fortune, when the darkness would rule the night and the day, and the sun would disappear for a brief time. She felt a vibration rumble below her. It rose to the surface and shimmied through her. Oats and Wonder both swung their heads toward Mave.

"Ssha," she said.

Both horses waved their muzzles up and down, then went back to their munching.

Mave pressed her palms against the ground. *I'm here*, she said.

She let the charged bubbles flow up through her palms into her body. *Wherever I go*, Mave thought, *the Ssha will find me*. As that truth seeped into her, her resistance to them trickled out. The knowledge she could never be truly lost brought her comfort. No matter how strongly she might close her heart against them, they would nudge tendrils of vibration to seek her out and connect with her. Their life depended on it.

The next day when Turnip appeared at her cave entrance, she was ready.

He still wore his priestly sashes, two strips of crimson and violet crossing his torso, the ends frayed and dangling. He'd added a cap to his outfit: like the Gigante priests' caps it was cone-shaped, rising above his head into a peak. Turnip had added bells to his cap so that if he shook his head or jumped up and down they clinked.

"Mavealeph?" he called.

Mave stood only a short distance from him. She was close

enough that she could have tapped his shoulder. Puzzled, she said, "I'm right here."

Turnip jumped, startled. The bells on his cap softly jingled.

His eyes met Mave's. "Ah, now I see you," he said. He blinked as though trying to bring her more fully into focus. "Mavealeph, would you hold up your hand?"

She raised her hand into the gray light of the day. Both she and Turnip looked at it. It was transparent. Her stomach dropped. "I perceived this was happening but didn't quite believe it," she said softly.

Turnip stepped inside the cave and pulled Mave to the two stools where she and Tear once ate in companionable silence, gazing at the valley that spread below them and the ocean beyond.

"Let's sit," Turnip said.

The soft light from the day filtered in. Turnip took Mave's hands in his and examined them, turning them palm up then palm down. He let them go, then leaned back on his stool and surveyed Mave from her feet to her head.

"Like it or not," he said, "the Ssha will make use of you to ensure their ways live on. I don't think you are fully in our time anymore."

Words and anger like memories rose up in her but stopped in her throat. "Why?" she asked. "To what end?"

He shook his head. "I can't say for sure," he said, "but it must have something to do with what Sister Ssha said the day your mother brought her and Tear to the council chambers. Your mother translated for us after you left. The Ssha in their underground caves had not succeeded in communicating their ways to humans. Something shut them off after the Gigante invaded. Everyone except you. The Ssha believe they can make their ways known in people of other, future times. You're the

Ssha's go-between, assisting those they transform."

Mave thought of her nightly half-dreams, half-visions with the young woman and the structure she lived in and curious surroundings. She told Turnip of this. He nodded.

"Sister Ssha said the transition had begun." He picked up Mave's hand and held it up to the faint light coming in the cave entrance. "There seem to be some side effects," he said.

The sadness she had felt when her gentle Ssha friend had reclaimed Tear returned and intensified into a knife of pain in her center. Whatever life she was planning was over. There was no escaping her fate. Even that realization in itself was part of the Ssha way. Now she fully understood the image of the staked rabbit on the clay chip.

Turnip looked out over the valley. "More smoke." He nodded to a point below. "The Gigante must be conducting one of their sacrifices again. Their god is a demanding one," he said, smiling.

"And the Ssha aren't?" Mave asked. "What's the difference? The Gigante sacrifice a small animal, the Ssha take over a human's life. The Gigante burn, the Ssha use. Both have common ends—keep their ways alive and thriving."

Turnip patted Mave's hand and nodded, the motion causing the bells on his head to softly jingle. Once upon a time he had dared break a rule that said only women could do certain things. Now he was an idiot, at least for appearance's sake. His role gave him protection, but what toll did it take on him to so convincingly act like a half-wit? He had tried to serve the Goddess in his way, been punished for it, and even so had arrived back at his starting point: in deference to the Ssha, original source of the Goddess.

"We live to serve, I guess," Turnip said, "or be served, like my namesake." He smiled at his joke.

"What is your real name?" Mave asked.

"Luther." His gaze cut to the side when he spoke.

"How long since you've been called that?"

He tilted his head as he thought. "Not since I was a boy. I had just come into my body when I couldn't resist the urge to attempt what only hieros house women could. I knew I would never be in line for consort, and I wanted that connection to the Goddess and the Ssha power."

Mave looked out over the valley's plains and beyond to the ocean. "I can stay here in my cave and assist. I accompany a young woman in her nightly border crossings. She doesn't seem to know that's what she's going through. If there are more like her who appear in my nightly visions, I'll accompany them too. But the Ssha can't force me to physically leave this cave. Even they don't have that ability."

Turnip looked at Mave, fear in his eyes. "Don't say such things. They will make it exactly so."

Mave laughed. She felt suddenly cheerful. "Let them try," she said. "What else can they do to me?"

After Mave and Turnip ate a small meal of hard bread and olives, Turnip rose to leave. "Will you come to the Gigante service tomorrow? They are saying it will be about our Goddess and their God."

"Again?" Mave asked.

He laughed. "True enough. But this time the Gigante aren't promising any sort of blending of our beliefs. They've made some decisions, they say, and will be announcing them."

"Would this be the Ssha getting me to leave my cave?" Mave asked, smiling. "I can come, but won't I alarm people in my half-visible state?"

"Stay shrouded and keep your head down. You're a woman. Act ashamed and obedient. No one will notice you." He said goodbye and made his way down the path.

For the first time in a moon cycle, Mave rose with the sun.

The eastern horizon was rinsed in red. Mave stood at the cave entrance, intent on taking in the energy of the sun as Beatt had taught her so long ago. She stood with her arms at her side, looking out at the plains below and the town of Dia beyond. As the sun rose out of its red bath, so too did plumes of smoke from yet another Gigante sacrifice. The columns of smoke grew dark and greasy looking as the flames reached the fat of whatever creature they were burning.

Mave thought of her mother. She had a clear image of her mother pulling up to the sacrifice in her chariot and face plate with the other Maryannu warriors behind her. Mave fell into the scene in her mind. Her eyes remained open but lost their focus on what was actually in front of her. A gray veil stood between her and the scene of the sacrifice. She watched it as she had watched the young woman who lived in another time and place. No one on the other side of the gray veil seemed to be aware of Mave.

A boy in a ragged tunic and pants, both the color of mud, stoked the fire embers with a pole. He backed away as the Maryannu and their chariots drew closer in. Mave's mother, Audria, bent into her chariot and pulled out a figure that had once adorned the entryway to hieros house. They called the figure Baubo. She had large, full breasts, wide hips, and stood with her legs apart to show the petals of her opening. No human woman's opening looked quite like that, but Mave's people understood that Baubo was a symbol for women's lushness.

Her mother in her Maryannu disguise raised the figure of Baubo above her head and drew her arm back, preparing to throw it in the fire. The two Gigante priests ran in their black robes toward her. "Not now," one of them shouted.

Mave's mother growled. "When?"

"At today's service," the priest said.

"Not soon enough," her mother said to the raucous cheers of her fellow Maryannu. "We'll go now, but we'll be at the service, watching you." She wheeled her chariot around, followed by the other Maryannu. As she steered her chariot out of the enclave where sacrifices were conducted, she turned her head toward where Mave stood behind the veil and winked.

Oats nickering near the cave entrance brought Mave out of the trance. Mave turned toward Oats and let her eyes come back into focus. Oats nickered again and gestured with her head toward the meadow. Mave rose and followed her there.

Wonder lay on her side in the grass, her ribs heaving in labored breathing. Mave dropped beside her. Oats stood above Mave, watching. Mave lay her hands on Wonder's ribs. Wonder's heart beat wildly. Her eyes rolled back in her head. "Wonder," Mave whispered, but Wonder did not respond. Her heaving chest grew still. She was no longer with them. Mave sobbed and curled into Wonder's cooling body. Oats stood with her head hanging low.

Mave rose and stood head to neck with Oats. Mave tried to get Oats to come back to the paddock with her but she would not move.

"Oats," Mave said, running her hand along Oats' bony flank, "wait for me. I'll be back as soon as I can. I have to go down into the town."

Mave left her there, standing next to Wonder's still body. She would need Turnip's help to bury Wonder. He would be at the service.

Mave dressed quickly, pulling on the required head covering and a band of rope to keep it in place. She slipped on her sandals. The soles had worn thin, and the bottoms of her feet had grown tough.

She walked the trail down the mountain, across the plain, and stopped at Dia's border. She was the only one about; the service had started. She made her way to the shrine. As she neared it she saw the Gigante had made much progress. They had fleshed out the skeleton of a month ago. The outer walls and roof were now solid.

When she stepped inside the shrine, she was reminded of the structures the young woman from her vision spent her time in. There was no comforting sense of enclosure of old Dia's clay pods. Being inside those pods was like being inside an egg. Nor was there the airy brightness of the stone home Mave and her mother had lived in. In the Gigante shrine there was structure, rigidity and coldness.

Mave joined the people at the back of the crowd. The two priests Lewi and Levi stood at the front waving golden-colored balls that gave off a fragrant smoke.

Mother? Mave thought. *Where are you?* She looked around. There were no Maryannu present, but they could have fit in the wide aisle that ran from the back of the shrine to the elevated platform in the front. The stairs of the platform were covered in a ruby-colored fabric. The priests wore their crimson and violet sashes over their black robes. The former Executrix, now madam pig farmer, sat with Turnip on a bench in front of the seated townspeople. In the two front row benches sat the White Gigante, their torsos rising like tree trunks from the benches. Their blond hair was long and tied in the back with a scrap of leather. Mave knew there were more of them, at least twice as many as she saw at the front of the shrine, but she'd heard they never went out together as one group. That way, if anyone made a surprise attack, there were enough to fight and enough to carry on.

Mave felt for her vial of Naphtha oil in her pocket. When in doubt, she thought, start a fire. In her own fashion, she too had adopted Gigante ways.

Here, came a voice in her mind. It was her mother.

And here, Mavealeph, came a hiss from the thoughts of her Sister Ssha, her kind giant lizard friend.

And also here, came the reassuring voice of the being who had tried so hard to become other than what she was: Tear.

Before Mave could mind-verse with any of them, another voice: *You've grown, Mavealeph*. It was Beatt. Her heart leapt at the sound of her old friend's voice in her head.

Mave sent out tendrils of connection to each of them, trying to locate them. While she did, the priests lifted the cover off a raised brass plate big enough for a human of Mave's size. A thick metal arm held the plate aloft with three chains running from the arm to the curved plate. She could see its blackened bottom from where she sat.

A vision of the entrance to the Ssha's underground dwelling burst into Mave's mind, followed by the sight of her mother, Sister Ssha, Tear, and Beatt all standing there, looking out with an unfocused stare.

The whooshing noise of a fire starting jolted Mave back to her immediate surroundings. Flames jumped up in the brass bowl. Together, Lewi and Levi lifted Baubo from the floor. She was the size of a small Dia child. The priests tied a cloth around her eyes and the flowering petals of her opening. Levi raised a knife.

"Do not be like the whore or a disobedient wife," he said.

As usual, Mave was confused by what their priests said. What was a whore? How was a whore like a disobedient wife? What did either have to do with the Gigante religion?

Mave looked around. Most of the people around her wore looks of confusion, their brows furrowed, their heads cocked to the side.

The priest crashed a knife down on Baubo's face, smashing off her nose. "Do not believe in false gods or their idols."

Mave jumped with everyone else. Her confusion turned to alarm, as did everyone else's. They all sat ramrod straight, their eyes wide in shock.

The priests rolled Baubo into the fire burning brightly in the brass bowl. A collective gasp went up among the people in the back. The white Gigante rose from their benches, backs hunched as though hunkering down for battle, their hands poised above the knives tied at their belts.

The congregation members held their tongues and collective breath as Baubo burned. The fire slowly died, and Baubo was gone, murdered, reduced to ashes that rose into the air then fell for someone to sweep up later.

Two boys carried a table to the front of the ruby-covered platform. They jumped off the platform and retrieved a jug of wine and several loaves of bread. They put the jug and bread on the table then retreated to the side of the platform.

The Gigante filed out of their row and formed two lines on either side of the platform. The priests came to the edge.

"God Father will provide," Levi said.

The Gigante stepped up to the platform. They knelt before Lewi and Levi and opened their mouths like baby birds. The priests tore off chunks of bread and put them in the Gigante's mouths. To each Gigante a priest handed a jug. The Gigante tipped it back, taking a swallow of the wine.

When they were done, the priests gestured to those sitting at the back. "God Father will provide for you, too," the head priest said and waved them forward.

Mave's stomach rumbled. She had not eaten. She joined one of the two lines forming to receive drink and bread from the priests.

None of those from the back who now crowded at the priests' feet needed to kneel; they stood more than a head below the platform. The priests tossed the bread into the people's waiting mouths, as though feeding dogs. Mave took her turn drinking from the jug, and her sleeve fell back, revealing her nearly transparent hand. Neither priest noticed; they were busy keeping up with the stream of open mouths.

Mave handed the jug to the next person in line and made her way to the back of the shrine. She sat on the bench and rested her shoulder against the hard wall. She let her eyes lose focus. This came easily when feelings of sadness were so strong. She let her mind roam the hills outside the town until something pulled her in, anything that would have her—a rock, rose, pebbles of dirt in the irrigation channels. *Mother*, she called in her mind, *they've killed the Goddess.*

Ssh, came her mother's voice, crooning. *We'll leave this time, my dear*, she said. *We will leave our bodies behind. Remember that promise.*

Mave looked at her hands resting in her lap. She could see through them to the cloth of her shift. *Mother, I don't have much of a body left to leave behind.*

Go back to the cave, came the hiss of Sister Ssha's mind-voice. *More await you in other times.*

Mave leaned her head against the wall, not moving. She would enjoy her few moments of rebellion until fate whisked her away. She gazed out the window at the light the sun cast. Then it dimmed as the moon inched toward her rightful place in front of the sun, shadowing its bright light.

Mother, Mave called out in mind-verse, *I see the eclipse.* As the moon inched into place, her breathing softened and relaxed—cool, wonderful, eclipsing darkness.

She jumped when the Gigante leaped up, all of them at once, shouting in alarm, pointing toward the windows as the moon darkened the sun's light. One of them shouted at the priests:

"Appease God Father, now."

Mave raised her head off its resting place on the cool stone. Could the Gigante really be that ignorant about what was happening? she wondered.

The priests bent and spoke to the two boys who had carried in the table with the bread and wine. They ran outside and returned a few moments later. One of the boys carried a bleating lamb in his arms.

The head priest raised up his arms. "God Father is angry," he called out.

The Gigante shifted from foot to foot, their backs hunched, their faces set in scowls as they looked out on the parishioners, as though they were the sources of their God's anger.

The two priests whispered to each other, then Levi bent his head to speak in low tones to the boy carrying the lamb. The boy put the lamb down. The lamb ran bleating on its spindly legs toward the door behind the platform.

"You," said one of the priests, pointing toward a man and his young son near the front of the townspeople. "Bring your boy here."

The man and his son, both with skin as brown as Mave's had once been before her nightly jaunts into other times, walked up the aisle to the platform then climbed up to join the priests. The man and his son were smiling. It seemed they had been singled out for something. Their smiles said, finally, some luck.

The two boys stoked the fire in the brass bowl that was big enough to accommodate one of Dia's children.

Mave realized what the priests were about to do and felt in her pocket for the vial of naphtha oil. The priests took the young boy by his shoulders and guided him toward the flames in the brass bowl. When the father tried to reach for his boy, a Gigante leaped onto the platform and pinned his arms behind him.

"No," Mave shouted, and ran down the aisle and up onto the platform. As the moon obliterated the sun, she grabbed the boy from the priests and shoved him toward his father, still held by the Gigante.

"Take me," Mave shouted. In the few moments of darkness she tore off her head scarf and shift and stood naked and almost entirely invisible at the Gigante's altar. The vial of naphtha oil rolled out of her shift pocket and down to the edge of the platform.

For a moment it seemed her mother, Sister Ssha, Tear, and Beatt joined her at the altar. They linked arms in front of the priests' fire. As they did, the father broke out of the Gigante's hold, yanked his son off the platform and ran toward the back of the sanctuary and, Mave hoped, out the door.

The moon slowly moved off the sun, and light returned to the sanctuary. The vision of Mave's mother, Sister Ssha, Tear, and Beatt linking arms in front of the priests' fire began to fade. Briefly, Sister Ssha's dimming outline became stronger, dancing with dots of color. Her image rose up, taller than the Gigante.

"Zet," Levi shouted, pointing at Sister Ssha's shimmering image towering behind them. "The fallen angel returns with his evil darkness."

Everything is drama with the Gigante, thought Mave. She wouldn't add to it. She walked to the edge of the platform, picked up the vial of naphtha oil, then jumped off and walked down the aisle, side-stepping frantic Gigante and townspeople. Turnip appeared at her side as she left the shrine.

"You leave a wake," he said.

Mave looked behind her. She had stirred the air and left behind glittery moats of dust.

"You also seem to have an almost-invisible follower," Turnip added, pointing to Mave's transparent, horned breast who trotted beside her.

Mave looked down at the cat-like being. The being turned his furry head up to glance at Mave then back at the path in front of them.

Mave's glittery trail caught the eye of the few townspeople who weren't wailing in fear with the priests inside the shrine. Mave headed to the border of Dia, invisible and naked with her trailing cloud of bright bits. Turnip followed at a distance, as did a few of the townspeople.

Mave walked across the plain and up the mountain to her cave. Her transparent horned beast faded as they neared the entrance. Mave turned and called out to Turnip, who stood below with a small crowd of townspeople.

As Turnip climbed up to the entrance, Mave pulled her shift over her head.

"Would you take care of Wonder's body?" Mave asked. "She passed this morning."

Turnip nodded. "I'll make a fire. The priests and the Gigante will be happy. They'll think we're performing a sacrifice to their god, purifying the mountain. That should keep you safe for a while. I'll take Oats with me back to the Executrix pig farm. Oats will be safe there and can live out her remaining days."

As Turnip left and walked toward the meadow where Oats stood, one of the townspeople waiting below climbed up with a fistful of yellow flowers. He placed it at the mouth of the cave, then climbed back down to the others.

Mave stood in the coolness of her dim cave, looking out at the now-bright day and the retreating backs of the townspeople, Turnip and Oats hurrying down the mountain to join them. Turnip kept a hand on Oats' neck. Smoke rose from the meadow. Oats swung her head back toward Mave where she stood near the cave's entrance. Oats nosed the air then turned to face the path down the mountain, letting Turnip guide her. She did not look back again. She too seemed to know she couldn't escape her fate.

14
Beast

SHE MOVED LIKE SMOKE, A smear of gray. When she squatted at the latrine, she deposited no more than a cindery smudge. The leaves she gathered and laid in the cave went to waste; the moon's fullness came and went with no response from her body, a husk. Mave's spirit went where it was called; she was no longer anchored by Tear's scent, warm skin, and lively stem. Mave's fury lay buried, as useless as the gold quartz lining the walls of the cave and the vial of naphtha oil still unopened in her pocket.

She no longer needed to forage for food or collect water. Visitors left loaves of bread, chewy roots, fruit, and olives at the cave entrance along with jugs of water and the occasional flask of wine.

Each night and now during the days too she split like a seed and opened up, providing a gateway between humans and the Ssha. Humans beyond Mave's time were distressed when they received Ssha energy. Their lives seemed as structured as the hard, ungiving walls of their dwellings. Every brittle thing shattered when Ssha energy entered people, and then they fell apart.

Mave always came back to the young woman from her first venture into other times. Her name was Rowena. She was slightly older than Mave and had fully blossomed into womanhood. Rowena seemed as wild as Mave's mother who, last Mave had seen, lived the life of a Maryannu warrior. Rowena drove her chariot as hard as Mave's mother drove hers, though Rowena's was enclosed and not powered by horses that Mave could see. Rowena moved from where she lived on a coast, near the crashing breakers of sea water, to a land-locked place with both trees and tall, hard-looking structures, more versions of the Gigante shrine. Rowena's new home was as white and cold as the Gigante's.

The Gigante didn't have to spread stories about the Goddess they'd splintered; she became a myth. A small group of mystics kept an intermediate realm alive, where the invisible lived, but the belief had to go deep underground to survive, not the physical deep of the Ssha subterranean caves but the imaginal deep where the only way in was through the organ of the imagination.

Staked like the rabbit she'd drawn on a clay chip, Mave gave in to her fate, walking the borderlands between worlds, the one thing she'd always avoided.

One day Beatt visited Mave in her cave. But he didn't visit in his physical form; he wavered before her like a smoky version of himself.

"Beatt?" Mave asked.

A smile flitted across his face like a ripple in the water.

He responded to Mave in mind-verse. *My turn now*, he said.

Mave lay on the cave floor, looking up at his wavering figure, illuminated by the bright daylight filtering in.

There are others now functioning as portals, he said. *Not many, but enough so that you can rest.*

Mave laughed for the first time in several years, a hoarse bark. *That's all I do*, she said in mind-verse. *My body doesn't move very well anymore.* She held up her barely visible hand. The joints were knobby, red, and swollen. It was the same with her feet, knees, elbows, and neck.

You've sacrificed your youth and your health, Beatt said. *It's time for me to take a turn. The daughter of the young woman you assisted is also ready. With her, I'll manifest in her realm and help others being reintroduced to Ssha energy. In their time they need something they can see, touch, hear, and smell to believe a thing is real. A wise woman waits. Her name is Agnes. She is what hieros house women have evolved into—a nun, they call it. Sister Agnes has figured out how our transformation works and stands ready to help. I hope to return to our time with this young woman or maybe Agnes, but first I have to manifest in their time and aid to those who are taking in Ssha energy.*

They were both quiet for a moment. Birds chirped outside the cave as they nested. Another eclipse season was beginning. A tear rolled down Mave's cheek. She looked down. The solitary little drop of water moistened the cave floor.

Goodbye, Mave, Beatt said, *for now*. And then his smoky self was gone, dissolving into tiny particles then into nothingness.

Mave lay on the cave floor until nightfall. She continued to cry. The tears ran down her cheek and fell onto the cave floor.

At nightfall she rose like a mantid, her limbs stiff as sticks. With each step, lightning bolts of pain stabbed up her legs. She palmed the wall for support and shuffled to the front of the cave. She stood at the entrance. The bread and olives someone had placed there the day before were still there, along with a flask of what Mave hoped was wine. Then she noticed a sprig of rock roses, the pink flowers that grew among the boulders. They had not been there earlier.

A rustling came from the bushes. Mave stepped back into the cave. As she watched, Tear emerged. She stepped up to the cave opening and picked up the roses.

For you, she said to Mave in mind-verse, looking blindly into the cave's darkness.

Mave reached her hand into the moonlight. Stained with her tears, it had grown visible. She held out her arms to Tear, and she came into them and they stood together for a long time at the mouth of the cave. Both responded—each grew lush, and Tear grew hard. They did not move yet from their tight embrace. Then Tear took Mave's hand and slid it inside her trousers. Once again Mave's hand could encircle Tear's stem. Mave then ran her finger along Tear's folds of flesh and quickly found her bud, that pearl. She slid her hands out and then ran them up Tear's sides, pulling her against her. Mave curled her low back so Tear's hard stem pressed against her bud. When Mave could wait no longer, she pulled Tear into the back of their cave.

They woke to Turnip standing over them, hissing, "Get up! Hurry! The Gigante will be here soon."

Both Tear and Mave staggered to their feet. The gray light of the overcast day filtered in.

"Dress, quickly," Turnip said. "Take whatever you can carry."

Tear pulled on her trousers and shirt, and Mave pulled on her shift. The vial of naphtha oil was still in her pocket. She grabbed two head scarves, her trousers, top and short jacket, and a large head scarf to wrap it all up in. She pocketed her barka bag of clay chips and gypsum.

"They saw the smoke from the fire yesterday in the meadow," Turnip said as he hurried them toward the front of the cave.

"They saw me return with Oats, coming from the direction of the fire. I had to tell them something. I told them I was purifying the mountain, driving away spirits to make it safe for them. That was the only thing I could think to tell them that they might believe. They did. They've sent several Gigante and Maryannu. They'll be here shortly." His eyes met Mave's. "I don't know if your mother is among the Maryannu they've sent."

Turnip gave them both a little push out of the cave. In the gray dawn, the fleet of Gigante and Maryannu came toward them. Two Gigante men on their huge horses lead the group. The two priests, Lewi and Levi, came next, sitting sideways on their horses. A row of three Maryannu in their face plates brought up the rear.

Turnip, Tear, and Mave crouched down and made their way to the meadow. They climbed up the short incline to the grove above. Tear and Mave lay their things just inside the grove then lay down near the edge of the cliff overhanging their cave entrance. Turnip removed his conical hat with its bells and joined Mave and Tear where they lay hidden at the cliff's edge.

The Maryannu stayed at the foot of the low mountain as the two Gigante and Lewi and Levi climbed through the olive groves and onto the path to Mave and Tear's cave. Mave and Tear lay flat, pressing themselves against the ground. They dared not look down or out. Their eyes met as they listened. The Gigante first entered the cave, then, swearing, backed out and ordered Lewi and Levi to go in, grumbling about the short height of the cave. Even crouching, they were too tall to walk in, and they wouldn't crawl.

Lewi and Levi entered the cave, their black skirts rustling. The Gigante called out to them as they made their way deeper into the cave.

"What do you see?" thundered one of the Gigante.

"Nothing," came Lewi's faint voice. "Some bedding. A palm leaf broom."

Mave stared in dismay at Tear. She had forgotten to take their broom.

Then a faint gasp. Both the Gigante stepped back, poised to run. "What is it?" shouted one, "the spirits of the dead?"

The Maryannu's armor clanked as they drew to attention. Both priests staggered to the cave entrance, breathing hard, carrying handfuls of rocks

"Look!" said Levi, showing the Gigante the rocks in his palm. "Gold," he said.

The Gigante men drew in sharp breaths.

"Gold quartz," said Lewi. "But still gold," he said, hurriedly, when Levi glared at him.

"How much can you see?" one of the Gigante asked.

"Several more handfuls," Levi said.

"There is likely more," said the Gigante. "We'll just have to figure how to dig it out. Is there an irrigation work crew coming over tomorrow?"

"There is," answered the other Gigante.

"Let's try them out on mining," the Gigante said, "see what they can dig up for us. Lewi, Levi, count the pieces you have."

After a few moments of silence, one of the priests said, "Eight," the other, "Twelve."

"Good," said the Gigante. "Carry those pieces back with us."

The Gigante made their way down the path, the leather of their belts and shoulder harnesses creaking.

"Like he knows what eight plus twelve equals," muttered one of the priests below Mave and Tear.

"Ssh," said the other. "Let's catch up. I don't want to be left behind here."

"Neither do I!" shouted Turnip, springing to his feet.

Tear and Mave barely breathed and pressed themselves flat.

Turnip danced a jig, swept up his jingling hat, and ran down into the meadow and around to the cave entrance.

"Bad Turnip," said one of the priests, "were you up there all this time?"

"Up? What's up?" Turnip asked. "What's down? I know where we need to go so we aren't left behind!" Turnip giggled.

"Fifteen," said one of the priests. "That's what eight plus twelve equals. Not twenty. Okay, Turnip, lead us out."

At the sound of the wheels of the Maryannu chariots, Mave and Tear cautiously raised their heads. The Gigante, Lewi and Levi rode toward Dia on their horses, the Maryannu in their chariots, all under a weak sun hiding behind the clouds.

Mother, Mave called to the retreating Maryannu backs.

Daughter, her mother answered.

Mave's little horned beast materialized beside her. *Mother?* Mave asked the beast in mind-verse. Mave's beast stared blankly at her, slowly opening and closing his heavily lashed eyes.

Here, came her mother's voice, and, in her Maryannu disguise, raised her arm briefly in a fist as she and her fellow warriors thundered away from them on the plain.

Mave's beast disappeared. Tear and Mave crawled to the edge of the forest and gathered their things. They each carried a handful of belongings and a pack on their back. Mave fingered the vial of naphtha oil in her pocket.

"We could make Apollonoulous in half a day," Tear said. "We can get there before dark."

"I move more slowly now than I used to," Mave said.

"We can rest as we need. We can find a place to stay overnight, if you'd like," Tear said. "When we get to Apollonoulous, we can find Inna and Lat. They'll help us get settled. We can find an herbalist for you, to give you something for the pain. I can work the Gigante cart crew there. You can work on the dice game." Tear opened her palm. "We can trade with this," she said, showing Mave a fistful of gold quartz. "And this," she said, pulling out another handful, then another.

Mave laughed. "How did you manage to collect all this in our last few moments in the cave?"

Tear stood close to Mave, and she could smell Tear's warm body and her piney scent.

"I've been tucking it away for the future. The future arrived," Tear said, and kissed Mave. "We can buy plenty of palm leaf brooms." She pulled slowly away after another kiss. "We should go."

Mave held Tear's hands briefly, then withdrew hers. "You start, I'll catch up," she said. "I want to say goodbye to our home."

Mave stood at the cliff overhanging their cave and looked out over the plains and Dia one last time. Her horned beast appeared at her side. He nosed the air in his semi-transparent state and looked expectantly at Mave, his eyes moving back and forth between her pocket where she kept the vial of naptha oil and the departing Gigante, priests and Maryannu.

Her fingers curled around the vial and slowly pulled it out. "Now?" she asked her beast.

The beast nodded.

Mave threw the vial of naphtha oil on the stone path below and hobbled toward the forest. Her horned beast trotted alongside her, offering Mave his steady haunches. Mave ran through the forest with her pack bouncing and pain jabbing into her legs, shoulders and arms, even with her beast at her side. When the blast came, it threw Mave off her feet.

The spirits of the dead rose shrieking from the depths of the mountain and spun in tornados toward the retreating Gigante. At the sound, the Gigante spurred on their horses, and the

Maryannu lashed the horses drawing their chariots.

"Mave!" Tear shouted from the other side of the grove and crashed through the trees back to Mave.

Mave struggled to her feet, pulling herself up with low-hanging boughs. She broke off a dead branch to use as a walking staff and limped out of the forest on Tear's arm.

They resumed their slow walk to Apollonoulous. A shimmer manifested under Mave's hand, her beast adding his furry support. His haunches warmed the knobby knuckles of her hand, and her heart sang to hear the howls of the dead as they chased the Gigante back to Dia.

Epilogue

LEWI AND LEVI SAT WRITING side by side at their worktable, the tips of their quills scratching across the tightly drawn section of woven fiber.

Lewi sat back and rubbed his wrist. Levi finished with a flourish, a little lightning flash of quill activity in the air. Then he too sat back.

"I've titled it 'The Lizard Men of Revelations,'" Levi said. "What do you think?"

Lewi thoughtfully rubbed his forearm. "Too long. How about just 'Zet of Revelations'?"

"Then it's sounds like the story of Zet."

"We could take 'Zet' out," said Lewi, "and just call it 'Revelations'."

Levi pondered. "Revelations," he repeated, tasting the word as though it were wine. He nodded. "That's good. Yes, we'll call it 'Revelations.' Let's be sure we've referred to the Ssha as 'Zet,' then I think we're done. We don't need to detail their entire history; we can let one stand for all in this record of their downfall. Besides, one figure with dark, evil intentions is more powerful, don't you think?"

Lewi considered this. "True," he said. "But leave in the omens. Those should be enough on their own to put the fear in most people."

Levi nodded and stood to reach for the weighted end of the strip of fiber. "Ready?" he asked Lewi.

Lewi nodded.

Levi cut the strip of fiber with a small knife. While Lewi lightly held down the end, Levi detached the scroll bar, set it on the worktable and bent to roll the clean end back onto the spool sitting on the floor. Then he carefully wrapped the end of the fiber which held the conclusion of their book onto the scroll bar.

Lewi stepped to the end of the table where the scroll bar with their completed work sat. He grasped the two ends and held them firmly while Levi pulled his end taut and rolled the scroll bar toward the heavy spool of wound fiber in Lewi's hands. The ends of their scroll bars met and clinked.

"The end," said Levi.

Check out this exciting preview of Book II in the No Boundaries series...

Down
Book II
of the
No Boundaries Trilogy

DACE BANKS, EIGHT YEARS OLD, raised Barbie's arm to wave goodbye to Mom, who stood at the door slipping on her sandals. Dad sat on the couch with his feet on the ottoman, holding The Virginian Pilot aloft as he read. He'd taken time off from his job flying jets for the Navy in nearby Norfolk to take them on vacation to Virginia Beach's First Landing State Park.

Mom straightened and flipped the ends of her long, sandy hair over her shoulders. She tugged on both ends of the self-tie of her denim wrap skirt, like a parachutist checking that her harness straps were secure. "I think they're coming," she said. "The feeling is so strong, just like before, when they came to get me when I was a teenager living here."

Dad lowered his paper and grinned. "You mean before you

started dating me and I scared them off?"

"Yes, my sweet," she said, swooping in to kiss him. "It's true, my other-worldly friends stopped coming to call once you were in the picture. Maybe they've had you on probation since then, and now you've passed, and they feel it's safe to come back. The feeling is centered on the beachfront section of the park. I think I should go down there."

"Can I come?" Dace asked.

"Of course!" Mom said. "You're welcome, too, you know," she said to Dad, chucking him under the chin as he saw them to the door. "Not afraid of aliens, are you?"

"I'll stay and hold down the fort," he said and kissed her cheek. "Can't give the aliens a chance to abduct all three members of the Banks' family at once." He handed Dace his compass. "Good practice." He'd recently taught her how to navigate using a compass, the stars and the invisible lines that crisscrossed the earth. "Latitude and longitude," he'd said, and when Dace's forehead creased in confusion, he amended, "or just lat and long." He pronounced the g in long like the g in orange, just like her French teacher said the g in the word longue, which also meant long.

Dace pocketed the compass and held Barbie by the torso as she followed Mom out the door.

They followed the path from their cabin to the boardwalk that led them out of the woods and onto the beach. The sun was just setting behind the gray clouds.

At the shoreline of First Landing Mom and Dace stood facing the waves, their toes just out of reach of the of the ebbing tide.

Dace stood silently as Mom closed her eyes and lifted her heart to the ocean. After a moment, she sighed and opened her eyes. "Nothing." She shook her head. "I don't understand. The signal was so strong."

The sun inched down below the gun-metal waves. The lights of the hotels and homes that book ended the park's beach popped on like fireflies.

Mom rubbed her left brow, blinked, and turned her head back and forth. "I'm getting the pixels of light," she said.

Dace looked questioningly at her.

"An ophthalmic migraine," she explained. She covered her left eye with one hand. "Shoot. One's definitely coming on. I'm getting the fractured light in my side vision. Haven't had one of these for a long time. I used to get them after the visitors appeared to me. But why would one come before a visit?"

"Does it hurt, Mom?" Dace asked.

Mom shook her head. "There's no pain, just temporary blindness."

Dace's eyes widened.

"Oh, not to worry. The eye doctor said years ago they happen to some people. He said avoid bright lights if one comes on and get to darkness." Mom cocked her head, and to Dace it seemed her gaze went out of focus, as though she truly were not seeing anything. "If I relax and don't look too hard, it's actually kind of cool. This crazy multi-colored worm circles more and more tightly and takes over my vision."

Worry churned in the pit of Dace's stomach. "Mom!" Dace said, tugging on her hand. "Shouldn't we get to darkness?"

"Just a few more minutes." Mom held her hand over one eye, then the other.

The lights along the boardwalk came on in the deepening dusk.

"Oh dear," Mom said. "The pixelated worm is taking over. We'd better find some darkness." She turned and blinked at the sand and the woods beyond. "We'll head for Bald Cypress Trail, which I'm pretty sure is past the dunes and to the left."

Taking Dace's hand, Mom stumbled up the dunes then veered left as the sand gave way to a grassy path.

"Can you see the opening to the trail?" Mom asked Dace, squinting at the woods.

"There," said Dace, pointing a few feet away. She pulled her mother along the few feet of the path and into the dark, marshy woods of Bald Cypress Trail.

Under the marsh's tree canopy, Mom stopped and faced Dace. She blindly patted Dace's arms, then her shoulders.

"Are you okay?" She cupped Dace's face. The ocean shushed the shoreline.

Dace placed her hands over her mother's, pressing their warmth into her cheeks, as her eyes adjusted to the gloom.

Dace paused, considering what Dad would say. "I'm fine," she said.

Dace didn't mind the dark, but her ability to sense presences did. She felt the heartbeats of the nocturnal creatures waking up to the dark.

The golden eyes of a critter low to the ground winked at Dace from the bushes. Another paired joined them, then a third.

Dace's heart raced. She patted the pocket with Dad's compass. Still there. She secured Barbie by the ankles. "Mom, I know what to do," Dace said.

"What, honey?" Mom asked.

Dace slid Barbie's head under Mom's palm. Her mother wrapped her hand around Barbie's plastic head with its bouffant of black hair and held it, considering. "How would Barbie get us home?" she asked. "Maybe we should just stay here in the cypress grove until the migraine passes."

The golden eyes winked out all at once. Something rustled on the other side of the trail, only a few feet from them.

"Not Barbie, Mom, the star; the star can get us home," Dace

said. "Dad taught me how on our first night here, when he taught me about directions and latta—" She paused. "Lat and long," she finished.

She turned and pointed to the sky beyond them which was framed by the entrance to the trail. Her mother looked without seeing. Dace dropped her arm. "If we can get back to the beach, I can find Polaris. Where we're staying is south of the beach. Dad told me. We just need to find Polaris, turn in the opposite direction, go down the boardwalk and after three cabins go right, and we'll be at our cabin. Here," Dace said, again taking Mom's hand and curling her fingers around Barbie's head. "You hold Barbie's head, and I'll hold her feet. I'll lead us home. Just follow my footsteps."

Her mother sighed. "I was so certain we were meant to be out here tonight. But so be it. It wasn't meant to be." She grasped Barbie's head. "Ready."

Dace turned back to face the path leading out of the woods. She kept a light hold on Barbie's feet resting on her shoulder as she stepped carefully along the well-groomed path, her mother's cautious footsteps behind her.

When Dace cleared the woods, she paused to find the Big Dipper constellation then followed its southern edge up to the tip of the handle of the Little Dipper—the North Star. At the sight of it, something deep inside Dace relaxed.

"How're we doing there, cap'n?" Mom asked.

"I found Polaris," she said. "I can get us home."

"Lead on," Mom said. "I sure can't. What a crazy light show I've got going on behind my lids."

Dace kept her eye on Polaris as she trudged through the dunes with her mother close behind. Dace envisioned the invisible lines that crisscrossed the earth, lines her dad and satellites used to navigate. *Lat and long, lat and long, lat and long*, she repeated silently to herself.

"I'm a little sad," Mom said. "I thought sure something was going to happen tonight. I wouldn't have brought you out here if my intuition hadn't been so strong. Still is. Now your dad has another reason to not believe in these things, and you'll be on his side, two against one."

Dace slogged up a dune. Grains of sand ground like tiny diamonds into the skin under the straps of her Jelly sandals. Dace liked that her mom aligned her with her dad. They could be a team. "Mom, no," Dace said, "It's better than that. It's two to watch out for you."

They climbed up the crest of the dune.

"Wait, Dace," Mom said, coming to a halt. "I'm sensing something." Her voice dropped to a whisper. "I knew we were supposed to be here tonight."

Dace turned to face her Mom, who nosed the air, her eyes still closed.

"Mom, come on, no." Her legs trembled and her stomach hurt. "There's nothing here. Let's just go home."

What would Dad do? Dace stared out at the dark shoreline beyond her mother. A twinkle in the spindrift caught her eye. Instead of falling back with the spray, it grew into a glittering shape. Dace stood very still. The shape, not far from where she and her mother had stood, took on the figure of a person. As the shape solidified, the outline suggested the broad-shoulders and slim hips of a creature about as tall as her father. The shimmering shape swung back and forth at the waist, as though enjoying a new physical freedom. A long tail of hair bound at the back of the neck swung as well. Then the shape came to stillness. The hollows of his eye sockets glowed with diffuse light. He directed his gaze at Dace and Mom. Alarm sounded in the pit of Dace's stomach then spread to her legs and arms.

"Dace," Mom whispered, "What is it?"

Lat, long, lat, long, Dace said frantically to herself, then the feeling that her head might blow apart calmed.

The waves continued their noisy crash on the beach. The foam from the breaking waves eddied up and back. The spindrift was again just saltwater spray.

"Nothing," Dace told Mom. "I didn't see anything. Just the moon on the surf. Hold on to Barbie's head, Mom, I've got to get us home." Dace turned back to resume leading them out of the dunes and beach grass.

Once they reached the boardwalk, the warm lights of the cabins glowed through the trees. Their cabin was three beyond these first two, off a little jog in the boardwalk. Dace looked over her shoulder to double-check Polaris was still at her back.

"Honey," Mom said, "Wait for a minute." She released her hold on Barbie's head.

Dace turned, dangling Barbie by the feet.

A beaming smile broke over Mom's face. "I can see!" she said. "The blindness cleared up just after I had that sense something was there."

"Nothing was there," Dace said. "I looked."

Mom stepped alongside Dace and placed her arm around her shoulders. "I guess I'll never get you or your dad to believe in what I sense," she said.

Dace edged away from Mom and faced Polaris with arms extended fully out.

"What are you doing?" Mom asked.

"What Dad taught me. My nose knows Polaris is north. Opposite is south, and my writing hand is east."

"What about west?" Mom asked, grinning.

Dace shook her head. "Dad hasn't taught me west yet."

"You're such a good little worker," Mom said, hugging her. "I think you and I have had enough lessons for one night. Let's go home."

Dace felt proud and grounded. I'm a good worker, she thought, as she reached for her Mom's hand and guided them along the boardwalk, counting cabins.

She halted. "Mom," she said, turning to look up, "you said home."

Mom laughed. "I'm sure I meant our vacation rental. It's not home, I know, not really, not yet." She clapped her hand over her mouth.

"Mom!" Dace said. "What? Do we have to leave Norfolk?"

"I wasn't supposed to tell yet," her mother said. "Your dad and a Navy buddy who's also getting out soon want to start a company to… hmmm, I'm not sure exactly how to say it, but basically figure out a way to develop and sell the system the Navy uses with satellites. It's what your dad and the other pilots use to navigate. Your dad says there are lots of other uses, and the military has said it's okay to develop it so civilians can use it. And your dad and his buddy can make and sell what they develop."

Dace led them quickly now along the boardwalk and turned right at the third cabin. Dad's energy radiated toward her like a beacon. She could never tell Mom or Dad that she felt things like this. Her mother would be overjoyed she was following in her footsteps and would then set out to homeschool her in her magical beliefs, and she would lose her newly defined, special connection with Dad: protecting her mother.

"Come on, Mom," Dace said, breaking into a trot, pulling her mother along with her, and then there was Dad, running toward them, his boat shoes pounding on the wooden slats of the boardwalk. His white shorts and peach short-sleeved, collared shirt glowed against his burnished skin. The door of their vacation cabin stood open behind him, bright light spilling onto the doorstep and the dark yard.

"There you are!" he called. He sprinted the last few yards between them and threw his arms around her mother.

Her mother gathered Dace into the hug.

"I got us home, Dad," Dace said, her voice muffled by her mother's skirt.

"God, Rowena, what took you so long?" Dad said, pulling back and holding her mother's face in his hands. "I was just about ready to have the park rangers start a search."

"I got one of those ophthalmic migraines down on the beach, and, you know, I can't exactly see when that happens." She closed her eyes and pressed her head into her husband's palm. She opened her eyes. "The only fix, darkness, didn't work. But Dace got us home." Mom stroked Dace's hair, long and sandy colored like Mom's, textured like Dad's.

"Dad, I remembered what you told me about Polaris," Dace said, tilting her head back to look up at him.

"Good girl," he said, looking down at her and briefly cupping the side of her head. He turned back to look into her mother's eyes. "You gave me a scare. Am I going to have to restrict you to base?"

Her mother laughed. "If you must, but first let me go to the Association for Research and Enlightenment, you know, the A.R.E., to find out what jobs are available."

For the second time that evening her mother clapped her hands over her mouth.

"I did it again!" she said, burying her face in her husband's neck. "I'm not good at keeping secrets."

"We know, don't we, Dace?" Dad grinned at Dace and squeezed her mother in a hug.

When he released her, he took Dace's hand and her mother's

and led them back to their rental.

"If you keep working hard to learn more about the stars and lat and long, Dace, they'll always get you to safety." Dad paused in the doorway to let Dace and her mother file into the house. "And safety is family, and family is everything." He closed the door with the three of them inside his temporary castle.

Dace tugged off her Jelly sandals, then trudged up the stairs to the cabin's second floor and her bedroom under the eaves. At the top of the stairs, out of the light, she turned back to say goodnight. Her parents hadn't moved from where they stood facing each other in the front door alcove.

Mom clasped her hands behind his neck, her arms a garland resting on his shoulders "I think I have to correct you on something," she said. "True love is everything. Everything follows from that."

Dad, smiling, gazed silently into her mother's eyes and softened against her, like melting ice cream.

Whenever Dace's mother spoke of love, especially if she was touching Dad, which was often, he became quiet and he lost his good posture. Those were her mother's moments of true power over Dad, it seemed to Dace. Was that why true love was everything? Dace wondered, because it had the power to take away another person's speech and ability to stand up straight? She turned away and tiptoed to her room where her lamp in the shape of the planet Saturn, pink with blue stars, glowed softly.

She folded Barbie at the hips then bent her plastic knees and seated her on the edge of the nightstand. The Saturn lamp glowed behind Barbie, and her cheerful smile shone out at Dace. Dace eluded sleep's grasp for as long as she could, then her eyelids drooped heavily and finally closed. A pair of orbs like eyes winked on outside the glass of her window under the eaves.

About the Author

Karen Cavalli, née Lound, writes fiction and non-fiction. Her work has been published online and in books and has won awards including Outstanding Secondary Science Book. She is a graduate of Old Dominion University where she earned a B.A., and The University of Alabama's MFA in Creative Writing Program where she studied with Margaret Atwood. She has worked in technology for over 10 years. She taught a writing course on the topic of psychological descent at the University of Minnesota and in North Carolina. Her work in technology has taken her to India and China and allowed her to work with individuals in Mexico, the United Kingdom, Australia, New Zealand and the emirate of Dubai. She loves her local Savage library and volunteers there. She is married to Tom Cavalli. She can be contacted at kcgoodguide@gmail.com

CPSIA information can be obtained
at www.ICGtesting.com
Printed in the USA
LVHW020503240720
661389LV00011B/171